By Ruth Fitzgerald

Emily Sparkes and the Friendship Fiasco
Emily Sparkes and the Competition Calamity
Emily Sparkes and the Disco Disaster
Emily Sparkes and the Backstage Blunder

Emily Sparkes and the FRIENDSHIP fiasco

by Ruth Fitzgerald

LITTLE, BROWN BOOKS FOR YOUNG READERS

To Dali and Edie for endless inspiration

LITTLE, BROWN BOOKS FOR YOUNG READERS

First published in Great Britain in 2015 by Little, Brown Books for Young Readers
This paperback edition published in 2015 by Hodder & Stoughton

7 9 10 8 6

Text copyright © 2015 by Ruth Fitzgerald
Illustrations copyright © 2015 by Allison Cole

The moral rights of the author and illustrator have been asserted.

A CIP catalogue record for this book
is available from the British Library.

ISBN 978-0-349-00182-1

Typeset in Minion by M Rules
Printed and bound in Great Britain by
Clays Ltd, Elcograf S.p.A.

The paper and board used in this book are
made from wood from responsible sources.

MIX
Paper from
responsible sources
FSC® C104740

Little, Brown Books for Young Readers
Hachette Children's Group
Part of Hodder & Stoughton
Carmelite House
50 Victoria Embankment
London EC4Y 0DZ

An Hachette UK Company
www.hachette.co.uk

www.lbkids.co.uk

CONTENTS

CHAPTER ONE

Worries, Wales and Wavey Cats

Monday evening

You're feeling so excited,
You're in a happy whirl,
And all because you have
A lovely baby girl.

Best wishes, Jenny and family X

No idea who they are.

The baby now has sixteen cards, which is four more than I got for my birthday. This is what they say on the front:

Eleven say: "It's a Girl!" (We know that.)

Three say: "Baby Girl!" (We know that too.)

One says: "New Baby!" (They probably bought the card early.)

And one says: "It's a Boy!" (From Great Auntie Audrey – bonkers.)

I can't believe Mum put the Baby Boy card up. She says it's funny. Confusing, more like. It's bad enough the baby not having a name yet. She's four days old now; Gran says you only get two weeks. Soon she will be illegal. Me and Gran are getting quite concerned. I have tried to explain to Mum and Dad they could be arrested if they don't decide on a name soon, but they're both a bit stressy at the moment. Dad says they've got "sleep deprivation" because the baby keeps waking up at night. Probably because she's wondering what her name is. I don't suppose they've considered that she might be having nightmares about going to school and just being called "Girl". She will have to walk into class and everyone will say, "It's a girl! It's a girl!" (or, "It's a boy!" if Great Auntie Audrey's involved) and she won't be able to tell her parents because they'll be in prison for not naming their child.

Of course they did manage to give me a name. Eleven years ago they decided to call me – wait for it, it's so exciting – *Emily*. I mean, really. I could understand if I was child number eight or something and they'd run out of ideas but their first ever baby and that's what they came up with. Talk about lack of imagination!

There are six Emilys in my school: Emily S. (me), Emily G., Emily C., Big Emily B., Small Emily B. and Other Emily B. (some people call her "Weird Emily B." but I don't.) Having the same name as everyone else is a total nightmare. If we're in the playground and someone calls "Emily", six different games have to come to a stop while everyone looks around to see which Emily is being called. As we also have two "Emmas", if someone is stupid enough to just shout "Em!" you may as well give up on break for the rest of the afternoon.

Mind you, I don't think weird names are much good either. Troika O'Mahoney-Turpin in Year Three probably spends more actual time telling people how to spell her name than she spends eating hot dinners (actually she has packed lunch, but you know what I mean).

So, to help Mum and Dad along, me and Gran are making a list of interesting, but not freaky, names for them to choose from:

gran's choices:
Diana (dead princess)

Kate (alive princess)
Carole (weather girl on breakfast telly)

My choices:
Bella (my best friend)
Hermione (yes, I am very good at spelling)
Harry (just in case there's been a mix-up and Great Auntie Audrey is right after all)

But they still haven't chosen. It's getting desperate.

Gran just texted me:

What about Cheryl?

She must be watching *The X Factor* again. She only really watches *The X Factor* and *Poirot* and I already said no to putting Agatha on the list.

I do actually have a secret name for the baby. I call her Yoda. He's in *Star Wars*. If you have a dad like mine you will know all about *Star Wars*. If you don't know just imagine a small, bald, wrinkly sort of person and that's him. (Yoda, I mean, not my dad – though he's getting there.) Anyway my baby sister is totally Yoda-ish.

By now you are probably thinking that I have a lot to cope with for an eleven year old. But there are a lot worse things than nameless babies and useless parents. Like the *really, utterly, completeliest* bad thing which is: my best friend, Bella, has moved.

To Wales!

Yes, Wales. As in *another country* (unless you live there of course, then it's not). Her mum and dad have bought a farmhouse and are going to make goat's cheese. She has been gone a whole three weeks. I have talked to her on the phone once or twice but Mum says it is very expensive to keep phoning abroad. Life without your best friend is like chips without tomato sauce, or pasta without pesto, or even sushi without rice I suppose, depending what level of food your family is on. My family is still really at chips level though my mum is always trying to push us more in the pesto direction.

Before Bella went she gave me a little white china cat with a wavey paw. It is a Japanese good luck symbol. I keep asking it to bring Bella back but so far it doesn't seem to be doing its job very well.

Every evening at six o'clock I meet up with Bella on the computer for a chat. I tell her how boring it is here and she tells me how cool it is in Wales.

Tonight's chat:

Bella says: Hi. Wales is cool. It is raining.

 Emily says: Hi. Boring at school without u. Dad fell asleep and forgot to pick me up so I had to have a lift home with Mrs Lovetofts.

 Bella says: Bad luck. What's happening at school?

 Emily says: Amy-Lee Langer got in trouble for snapping Zuzanna's dolphin rubber in half!

 Bella says: OMG! I loved that rubber.

 Emily says: I know - it was the best rubber in class. But

8

I don't really care because I
don't like Zuzanna.

 Bella says: Oh yes - I forgot.

 Emily says: U r forgetting
about me already! Can't u get
yr mum and dad to change their
minds and come back?

 Bella says: They love it!
Tomorrow goats are arriving.
And I started my new school
today!!!!

 Emily says: Oh no!

 Bella says: It was OK. Everyone
is Welsh. And guess what! I am
sitting by a girl called Emily!

 Emily says: Noooooooo! I am
sitting by Wavey Cat - I put

him on your side of the table
every day.

 Bella says: Here is a sooooo
cuuuuute picture of a bunny to
cheer u up.

 Emily says: Oh soooooo
cuuuuuute!!!!

I wait for a few minutes but Bella doesn't say
anything else.

I should have ended with a question.

CHAPTER TWO

Eco-Disaster

Tuesday morning

I have given in and put Agatha on the list. I suppose it's better than no name at all, but I'm not hopeful. I can't even get Mum and Dad to look at it at the moment. It's like having zombie parents. They are taking absolutely no responsibility for me. This morning I had to get my own breakfast, find the remote (which was not easy as Dad had put it on the phone charger), turn the TV to the right channel *and* open the curtains in the living room. Then there was no school uniform washed so Mum actually got it back out of the washing basket.

She said, "You don't have to have clean clothes every day you know."

Like we're in Tudor times or something! I told her it smelled and I wasn't going around in a cloud of baby sick all day so she stuck it in the tumble drier with a sheet of Bounce. After that it just smelled like a baby had been sick in a spring meadow but there was no more arguing because she was feeding Yoda and for that she needs "total calm" or the baby gets excitable milk and won't sleep again. (Dad gets the same thing with coffee.)

I think Mum wishes we *were* in Tudor times. She doesn't like anything modern any more. Since getting pregnant she has gone completely environment-crazy.

She said, "This time around I am going to do everything right."

Which makes me worry what she got wrong the first time.

So that she'll grow up environmentally friendly, Yoda's bedroom is all wood and organic stuff. Gran says organic wasn't invented when she had her babies but they turned out all right. Anyway, Yoda's not allowed to sleep in her own room yet. Really it's a waste, especially when we haven't got an actual playroom anywhere in the house. I am sure I am the only person I know who hasn't got a playroom, well apart from Gracie and Daniel ... and Babette and Nicole ... and Joshua Radcliffe, but he lives in a yurt (which is a big tent like you have on holiday – but they're not on holiday so it's not normal at all), and anyway, he's probably got a play-yurt.

Amy-Lee Langer (total class-bully-type person) says her new baby sister's room is "pink absolutely everything". Bella says that's totally sick-making, but it's OK for her to say that, even Amy-Lee Langer can't get her in Wales. Mum doesn't agree with pink. Yoda's room is painted in "Pale Bamboo" (really it should be called "School Lunch Cabbage"). Mum says it's "calming".

I think Mum should put "Pale Bamboo" in her room too. She got very stressy when Dad said he was going back to work today but like Gran says, it's all very well her having babies but somebody's got to pay the bills around here.

The worst thing Mum has done eco-wise though is sell her car. It was only a small one so I'm sure it wasn't destroying much of the planet. She says she's going to use the money to buy a smart baby buggy. She said she wants a proper one this time and not "a second-hand rust bucket" like I had.

"You don't need to sell your car, love," Dad said. "I'm sure we can afford a hundred pounds or so."

"A hundred pounds!" Mum said. "That won't get us one wheel of anything decent. I want a Baby

Eco-Jogger Deluxe! Then I can go running with the baby and get fit. I could even jog down to the market. Who needs supermarkets? Who needs a car?"

I was nodding and smiling at her for the sake of a peaceful life when I had a disturbing thought. "But, Mum, if you haven't got a car, how am I supposed to get to school?"

"Walk," she said, as if this was a perfectly sensible idea.

It takes twenty minutes to walk to my school! By the time I get there I won't be in a fit state to learn anything. Anyway we are usually late even with a car.

I told Gran about the walking thing and she said Mum was "playing fast and loose" with my safety "for the sake of a few trees".

When I told Mum this she said, "Fine, I'll walk with you – it will do us all good." She has an answer for everything, even Gran.

Luckily we don't have to start the walking thing till next week as Mum hasn't managed to get round to buying the Baby Eco-Jogger Deluxe yet and – double luckily – Dad's going to take me to school till then in his van.

I like Dad's work van – it's quite smart and has a personalised number plate: L33K 5RS. It's supposed to say "Leaks R Us", which is the name of the plumbing company he works for, but they couldn't get the A, so it sort of says "Leeks R Us". Dad says it doesn't matter but I think this could be very confusing for people who might think they are getting a delivery of vegetables. Especially if the leak was in the kitchen.

I went to Dad's office once and I asked his boss if there were ever any problems in this area, but he just said, "Oi. Who brought a flaming kid in here!" so I'm none the wiser really.

Anyway Dad is in a very good mood this

morning. It's his first day back to work since Yoda was born and he has been whistling the whole way.

Everything is fine till I am just getting out of the van at school, then he says really quickly, "By the way, Gavin's mum is bringing you home this afternoon." As if it is perfectly responsible to allow your child to be collected from school by any random person who happens to have a spare seat.

I am only halfway through saying, "Are you mad? I'm not going home with Gross-Out Gavin!" when he drives off.

CHAPTER THREE

Dead Dolphins
and Sworn Enemies

Still Tuesday

I get into school and there is the usual fuss and
racket going on. Gracie McKenzie's packed lunch
has exploded over Daniel Waller's Numeracy
homework and she is desperately trying to wipe
up a strawberry drinky yoghurt with her PE top.
Daniel is crying. He's *very* sensitive. Once he cried

all afternoon because he realised he had odd socks on.

I am trying not to think about Gross-Out Gavin but this is not easy as he and Alfie Balfour (who is just as annoying but at least his mum makes him clean his teeth) are having a loudest burp competition – into each other's faces. This is the sort of thing they do all day. *For fun!*

I get Wavey Cat out of my bag and put him on Bella's side of the table. He waves his left paw at me and I look at his little smiley face and feel sad and happy all mixed together.

Everyone is scrabbling about trying to find their homework. Our school has a new policy – homework *every* night. This is because we have a new head teacher, Mr Meakin, who is *completely* strict. Before Mr Meakin we had a Head Teacher Vacancy. This means they couldn't find anyone to be in charge so the teachers were allowed to run a bit wild. But that's all changed now. Mrs Lovetofts, our teacher, says it's a headache trying to keep on top of all the new homework, but I don't know what she's worrying about, she doesn't have to do it all, does she?

Amy-Lee Langer and Yeah-Yeah Yasmin are talking in the corner. Probably trying to come up with new and exciting ways to make people miserable. Well Amy-Lee is probably trying to come up with new ways and Yeah-Yeah Yasmin is just agreeing with her.

Nicole and Babette, the (not actually French, but their mum wants them to be) twins, are arguing about the Eiffel Tower colouring-in sheets for their club. They run their own lunchtime French club and force all the little kids to count to ten and say "*merci*" and "*bonjour*". Although I sometimes think that Nicole and Babette don't really speak a lot of French themselves, just what their mum makes them learn in the car on the way to school.

The biggest crowd though is around Zuzanna's table. She is showing off the little matchbox coffin she has made for her dolphin rubber.

"There will be a short funeral service today at lunchtime," she says. "I will be burying him behind the picnic tables."

"Oh, poor Dolphin!" says Small Emily B. Thank goodness Daniel Waller is still wiping his homework and hasn't heard or he would start howling all over again.

I could go and join in but I don't want to. It's too noisy today and I am not in the mood to discuss dead rubbers. Anyway I don't like

Zuzanna – at the start of term she had a birthday party and didn't invite me, and it was at Rollerworld! I was the only girl in the whole class who didn't get an invitation (well, except for Amy-Lee Langer and no one invites her to parties, not unless you really want to get in a food fight with the Rock 'n' Roller Chicken Dippers). Zuzanna gave out all the invitations at break time and I couldn't believe it when there wasn't one in my tray too.

Then when I was in the toilets I heard her say to Babette, "I'm not inviting Emily because she's a total pain."

So I didn't invite Zuzanna to *my* cinema party a few days later. Since then I have realised that she is very annoying and *very not* interesting so I probably wouldn't have gone to her party even if she did ask me. In fact she is now my sworn enemy. It is a total pity she is not nice, however, because her best friend, Mina Begum, also left last term and we could have sorted out each other's Best Friend Vacancy.

Except I don't want a new best friend anyway. I just want Bella to come back and sit in the empty seat next to me. I make Wavey Cat's paw move again, and I think, *If you could just get on with the good luck thing it would be great.*

The door swings open and in comes Mrs Lovetofts.

"Good morning class!" she says all bright and cheerful. "Welcome to another lovely day at Juniper Road Primary." She is always bright and cheerful which is not normal teacher sort of behaviour, I know, but she seems to get away with it. She is quite old and has lots of hair which is always escaping from her hairclips. She is not very good at controlling the class, so she is lucky that I am able to control myself. At least there is one less person for her to worry about.

"Homework books to the front please."

Straight away Amy-Lee Langer and Gross-Out Gavin shoot their hands up in the air.

Amy-Lee says, "I haven't had time to do it because I've been ill." What she means is she hasn't had time to bully anyone into letting her copy theirs.

Mrs Lovetofts says, "All right, Amy-Lee. Try to do it tonight." She is far too soft on her, it is no wonder Amy-Lee's behaviour problems are not improving.

Gross-Out smirks. "I didn't know we had homework, Miss."

"Why didn't you know, Gavin?"

"Dunno, Miss."

"But we have homework every night, don't we, Gavin?"

"Dunno, Miss."

"What were you doing when I gave out the homework?" Mrs Lovetofts says with a sigh.

"Dunno, Miss."

I can see this might go on for quite some time so I am looking around trying to find something to be interested in when I see – through the glass panel in the classroom door – Mr Meakin, the head teacher, standing outside. This is not unusual – Mr Meakin is the sort of head teacher who is always popping up in unexpected places trying to catch the teachers out for smiling too much or drinking tea in the classroom.

Then I notice the top of a blonde head below Mr Meakin's elbow. Mr Meakin opens the door a little bit and peers in. I am a bit worried for Mrs Lovetofts, in case she is looking too cheerful, but it is OK because she is just in the middle of saying, "What do you think will help you to remember, Gavin?" (As if she doesn't already know the answer.)

And now I can see that the blonde head under Mr Meakin's elbow is attached to a body and it is the body of a girl. She is wearing a red miniskirt and sparkly tights, which is not at all normal for a Tuesday.

She pokes her head into the classroom and says, "*This* is *Year Six*? Okaaaay. I guess I'll just have to get used to it."

Get used to it? This can only mean two things. Either she is a new girl or she is a new teacher who is really short and looks about ten. I am just thinking it is most likely that she is a new girl when Mr Meakin shuts the door again and they go off. Mrs Lovetofts doesn't even notice. Really she should be more aware of what is happening in her classroom.

I don't have any more wondering time left, however, as Mrs Lovetofts has given up explaining homework to Gavin (until tomorrow morning) and is now talking about Tudors, though I'm sure my mum could teach her a thing or two about sixteenth-century living conditions.

Mrs Lovetofts is very excited because we are going on a Tudor Times Time-Travel Trip next week. We are going to Ickwell Hall where, apparently, people hang about wearing costumes, pretending to be real Tudor people (although, I think, if they were doing it properly they would all be lying around pretending to be dead, because that's what the Tudors are).

It is a bit annoying because Ickwell Hall is only about twenty minutes away, and everyone knows the best bit about going on a school trip is the bus journey, but Mrs Lovetofts is very enthusiastic.

"Everyone will need a partner," she says, "as you will be doing a lot of work together on the day. It will be very exciting. Living history!" Everything makes Mrs Lovetofts excited – she gets excited about music lessons, assembly, school lunch. Once she even clapped her hands when Joshua Radcliffe was sick in class.

History is Mrs Lovetofts' favourite thing of all. Really I can't see the point of it. *Future* would be a better thing to learn about, then I could find out all sorts of things like: will my baby sister ever get a name? And: will Bella's parents ever come to realise that making goat's cheese is not normal for people?

I don't know who is going to be my Tudor Times Time-Travel Trip partner. I don't even want one. There is only Zuzanna spare and I am *not* being partners with her.

"Unfortunately Alfie Balfour won't be able to join us on the trip because he has to go and visit his nan in her special old people's home," Mrs Lovetofts says. (Alfie's nan is actually in prison for two weeks for refusing to pay her TV licence, it was on the news and everything).

"So," Mrs Lovetofts is saying, "that means Gavin won't have a partner. Now who can I pair Gavin up with?"

Too late I realise what disaster is about to happen! Mrs Lovetofts looks around the class and catches my eye. I know exactly what she is going to say.

"Ah yes, Emily Sparkes. You don't have a partner now, do you?"

"I ... Miss ... I ... " I just can't seem to make any proper words come out. Why has she picked on me? I don't want a partner and I definitely don't want Gross-Out Gavin!

Finally I blurt out, "But what about Zuzanna?" I look over to Zuzanna's table but it is empty. Then I see a pair of white socks and black shoes sticking out from under her chair. I have to admit she's quick – she must have made a dive for it.

"Who?" Mrs Lovetofts says. She is also very forgetful. "Oh yes, Zuzanna. Where is Zuzanna?"

Zuzanna wriggles out backwards and then stands up and gives me a seriously super-evil look (*worse* than a death stare). "Just dropped my pencil, Miss," she says.

"Oh yes. Very well then – you can be partners with Zuzanna," Mrs Lovetofts says.

"No way!" say Zuzanna and I together, glaring at each other across the classroom.

Before Mrs Lovetofts can say any more there is

a wail from the other side of the class as Daniel Waller realises he has forgotten his drinks bottle.

"Oh, never mind!" Mrs Lovetofts says. "We'll sort out partners tomorrow."

I have managed to avoid Gross-Out Gavin all day and I'm hoping everyone might forget about the lift home. Gavin is brilliant at forgetting. Homework, PE kit, nose-wiping, zipping up his trousers – you name it, he forgets it. I think if I just keep quiet long enough he might go home and maybe his mum will forget too. Then I could look all lost and abandoned in the playground and Mrs Brace the secretary will have to phone my mum and she will come dashing up to the school reception all red-faced and guilty, with the baby slung across her back in an old shawl. Mrs Brace will have stern words with her (all the parents are scared of Mrs Brace). I will forgive Mum of course, after a couple of days.

But I should know better. Mrs Lovetofts has just handed out the letter about the Tudor Times Time-Travel Trip when she picks up a note and says, "Oh yes, Emily. Don't forget you are going home with Gavin tonight."

There is a loud crash as Small Emily B. falls off her chair, and a bit of a fuss picking her up again.

"I mean Emily Sparkes," says Mrs Lovetofts.

The worst bit is when I hear Zuzanna giggle. I try for dignified and sensible. I look straight ahead and walk out to the cloakroom to collect my coat. Then I remember I haven't got a coat today because my parents have more or less abandoned me. So I walk out of school – to where Gross-Out Gavin's mum is waving to me from beside their PINK CAMPER VAN!

CHAPTER FOUR

The Van of Doom

Still Tuesday - unfortunately

Surely if my parents really couldn't get it together between the two of them to collect me they could have chosen someone with a less embarrassing mode of transport, like Father Christmas or Noddy.

Gross-Out thinks that his camper van is cool, but only because he has completely no understanding

 of anything. It is not even a tiny bit cool, it is really old and smells like mud and mushrooms. Gracie Mackenzie says it would be cool if it was a *real* Kombi – her uncle has a *real* Kombi and that is "totally ice cube" (Gracie knows about that sort of stuff). But Gavin's is not a real Kombi – so really, it's just an old van, painted pink.

Gross-Out comes running past, shoves me out of the way and clambers into the front seat, like sitting up front in an oversized Barbie bus is something you might actually want to do.

I am trying to climb into the back when his mum says, "No, dear. You have to get in the front with Gavin, on the double seat. I've got some floral tributes in the back."

I look through the back window and see at least

ten wreaths. Wreaths – as in *flowers for dead people*! And I'm thinking the only way you can know that many dead people is if you are really, really unfortunate – or a serial killer. I turn to look at Gross-Out's mum and for the first time I notice there is something a bit odd about her. She is very thin and with a beaky nose and her hair sort of lurks around her face.

I must go a bit pale because she gives me a funny look and says, "Don't worry, dear. I'm a florist. I'm stopping off at the funeral home on the way back."

What choice do I have? I have to take her word for it. I climb in and sit next to Gross-Out, so close I can almost hear his head lice chatting. I give another quick glance in the back and in among all the wreaths there is one shaped into the word "DAD". And I'm telling you, just for a second, I wonder how that dad died. Like maybe he forced his daughter to go home in a pink van with a load of funeral flowers and the school's grossest boy and his living-dead mother and, you know, maybe she just snapped.

Gross-Out's mum says, "They are for the funeral of an old chap, from the nursing home." She gives me another unconvincing smile and says, "Right, buckle up."

But now I can't get my seat belt on. This is because it is absolutely and totally ancient and not like anything people have in the modern world. It is probably the same type of seatbelt Noah put in the ark to stop his wife getting off again and saying, "Oh, seriously, Noah. A drop of rain never hurt anyone."

Gross-Out's mum has to lean in and do it up for me. Gross-Out waits till his mum shuts my door and is walking back around the van and says, all sing-songy, "Emily Sparkes always gets bad marks." This is what he always says to me. Like he is in Year Two or something (which is where he should be really).

"Why don't you buy a magnifying glass and see if you can find your personality," I say back, and I think it is quite a good line, but it is totally wrong timing because Gross-Out's mum has just opened her door. She gives me one of those looks with raised-up eyebrows and wrinkly lips and says, "Now then, Emily."

I can *feel* Gross-Out smirking. I would dig him with my elbow but that would mean actually touching him. So I give him the super-evils, which I learned from Zuzanna earlier, and he goes a bit pale. His mum gets in and slams the door, which I think is a pretty risky move given that it's only really made out of rust and dirt. Then it takes five goes to get the van started, and every time it sounds like a tumble dryer full of tin cans. In the end most of school are looking at us and they all cheer when it finally gets going.

Gross-Out's mum says, "Atta girl!" and slaps the steering wheel (which is another risky move in my opinion). Gross-Out even thinks *this* is cool and starts punching the air and giving thumbs-up signs to everyone. I am totally slumped down in the seat. Luckily there is a big yellow smiley face sticker on the window which I mostly manage to hide behind.

We drive past Nicole and Babette and I am very pleased that they are too busy arguing to notice me. I have to admit though I feel a bit more understanding about Gross-Out now. If he has to go through the pink van nightmare every morning and afternoon it's no wonder he has problems.

When Gross-Out's mum finally releases me outside the house I am faint with nerves. We had to drop off the flowers at the funeral home. This woman in a black suit came out to get them. She looked right at me and gave me a sort of creepy half smile that made me go all shivery and I couldn't seem to tear my eyes away from hers. If Gross-Out hadn't chosen that moment to burp really loudly I might have been hypnotised and forced to follow her back inside and never be seen again. It is the only time I have ever been grateful for one of his disgusting bodily noises. I rush upstairs to find Mum and tell her everything, but she is having a lie down "because the baby is sleeping". The fact that *I* am awake doesn't seem to be important.

Still she makes a half effort and says in a sort of mumbly way, "Nice day?"

"No," I say. "Gross-Out's mum tried to deliver me to a funeral home."

"Shhh," she says. "You'll wake the baby."

"I've got a letter about a school trip."

"Put it over there," she mumbles.

So I give up and go back downstairs to make a jam sandwich instead. There is no bread and no jam though, so I am forced to eat an apple. I decide to go on the Internet to see if there is anyone in the universe who wants to speak to me but there is a note stuck on the computer:

Do not use. Broken again. Sorry.
Dad

My life is turning into a complete disaster. My best friend has left, my parents are zombies, I have to be school trip partners with the most gross-tastic boy in class and I only have fruit for comfort.

CHAPTER FIVE

Who's that Girl?

Wednesday morning

"Hello, Year Six," Mr Meakin says. Everyone is quiet. Mr Meakin never interrupts our lessons. It is either a major telling-off or a tragic announcement. He likes to do those things himself. "I'm sure," he continues, "that Mrs Lovetofts has explained that we have a new starter today."

"I hadn't actually quite got around to that yet," Mrs Lovetofts says, smiling.

Mr Meakin does not look pleased. But then Mr Meakin never looks pleased. Unlike Mrs Lovetofts, he has learned the proper facial expressions to get on in teaching.

"This is Chloe Clarke, everyone," Mrs Lovetofts says as Mr Meakin goes out to do some miserable but important stuff in his office.

Chloe Clarke looks at everyone with a big smile and says, "Hi!"

I am surprised because most people don't really say anything much when they're new. She has very white teeth and blonde hair in a long plait. Her skirt is quite short and she has black tights with silver stars up the sides and shoes which are not the same as everyone else's. Joshua Radcliffe is sort of staring at her like he's seen an angel, but she doesn't look like the sort of girl who'd be interested in a yurt dweller.

Mrs Lovetofts says, "I'm sure you will all make her feel very welcome. Chloe, why don't you go and sit next to Emily?"

"But that's Bella's seat, Miss!" I say. Mrs Lovetofts gives me a little smile and I hear somebody giggle. I bet it was Zuzanna.

What if Bella comes back? Wavey Cat is supposed to bring me luck! I don't know why Mrs Lovetofts picked me anyway. Zuzanna has had an empty seat next to her for much longer than me – she should be first in line when it comes to sorting out new people. Mrs Lovetofts never thinks things through properly. I have enough to get used to at the moment with nameless babies and pointless parents and last night I couldn't even speak to Bella because the computer was broken. I am much too stressed to deal with smiley girls. But it is too late now.

Chloe swishes into the seat next to me and

says, "Hi, Emily. Nice to meet you," in a sort of American-ish (but it might be that she watches too much TV) voice.

I say, "Hi," in a way which I hope also sounds like "leave me alone".

Then she says, "Oh. What a cute cat," and reaches out to *touch* Wavey Cat's paw. I quickly grab him away and put him on my table.

Luckily Mrs Lovetofts has just decided to do a Tudor music lesson so I don't have to say any more to Chloe for a while and even if I did she wouldn't be able to hear me above Mrs Lovetofts singing "Greensleeves".

It is making it very difficult for me to concentrate on how to get out of showing Chloe around the school. I absolutely do not want to spend first break wandering about the school saying, "Here is the teachers' toilet," and, "This is a fire extinguisher."

By the time the bell goes for break I have decided to say, "Sorry, I can't show you round. I've got loads of pencils that need urgent sharpening," which I know is not the greatest excuse I've ever come up with but I am under pressure. But when I turn round I find Chloe is already walking around the class going, "Hi! What's your name?"

Before long everyone is chatting to her like she's been around for ages. The only person who is not hanging round her is Amy-Lee Langer. This is because she is on break-time detention outside Mr Meakin's office over the murdered dolphin incident.

Joshua Radcliffe says, "Welcome to the crazy class, Chloe!" But he's just trying to make us sound more interesting because it's quite an ordinary class really.

"Yeah. Yeah," Yeah-Yeah Yasmin says.

Nicole says, "Hi, Chloe. Welcome to Juniper Road Primary." She flashes her a big smile and then says in a showy-offy voice, "*Parlez-vous français?*"

And Chloe says, "*Oui. Bien sur.*"

"Oh, you are clever," Zuzanna says.

Chloe nods. "I used to go to Magnolia Hall. At Mag Hall we learned French from Reception."

Nicole's eyebrows spring up under her fringe – she looks at Babette in a very worried way. They have never had competition in the French area before.

Zuzanna says, "Is Magnolia Hall a private school?"

Chloe says, "Yes."

Gross-Out says, "Are you rich then?"

Chloe says, "Yes."

Alfie Balfour says, "Ri-ich, ri-ich, Chloe is ri-ich." And does a stupid gorilla dance.

Gross-Out says, "Then why don't you go to Magnolia Hall now? Lost all your money?" and he and Alfie start sniggering.

Chloe opens her mouth to say something but Zuzanna leaps in (to the conversation, not Chloe's mouth) and says, "Just go away, Gavin. Chloe doesn't want to speak to you." Then she says, "I so looove your tights – my mum will only let me wear white socks."

"Parents!" Chloe says. "Tell me about them. Like they are *totally* on another planet to their kids."

Zuzanna says, "*Totally, boatally,*" and goes all giggly.

And then Chloe goes all giggly too and they put their heads together and go all giggly together.

I am thinking I am so glad I decided to stay out of this and completely not be friends with Chloe Clarke because it is all just too childish, and even though Zuzanna is my sworn enemy, I am surprised she is joining in because she is usually more sensible.

Then Zuzanna says, "By the way, Chloe, have you

heard about the Tudor Times Time-Travel Trip next week?"

And I suddenly realise what is going on. Zuzanna is trying to make friends with Chloe – and I know why! Because if she is friends with Chloe then she will have a partner for the school trip and I won't and I will be the one to end up with Gross-Out! Well, Zuzanna Kowalski, you are not getting away with that. *Totally, boatally* not!

I grab Chloe's arm and say, "Well that's enough chit-chat. Time to *totally* show Chloe the school council noticeboard," and I steer her out of the door before Zuzanna even has a chance to finish the giggle she has started.

I just about manage to keep Chloe distracted till it's time for class again by showing her the highlights of the reception area like the "We Raised £41.34 for Polar Bears" certificate and the photo of the 2007 school football team getting a cup from someone who once played for Bolton

Wanderers. But it is not easy, she does seem to get bored very quickly. We get back into class just as the bell goes and I waste a few more minutes showing her the bit of doorframe where Mrs Lovetofts sticks all the spare Blu-tack and then we have to go and sit back down. Zuzanna is sitting in her chair across the class trying to smile at Chloe and give me the super-evils at the same time which makes her face scrunch up and look very strange.

By lunchtime I have completed a list to keep Chloe busy and out of Zuzanna's way (also it was more interesting than learning about Cardinal Wolsey).

Things to Show a New Person
 Girls' toilets (don't go in cubicle three –
it's haunted)
 Coat hooks (she won't have one yet, Mrs
L. always forgets, but she can use Mina

Begum's - NOT Bella's, in case she comes
back)

Water fountain (NEVER drink out of it!
Gross boys put their mouths over it.)

Trolley for putting packed lunches on
(right next to the heater so don't bring
yoghurts)

That should keep her away from Zuzanna for a
bit. I'll have to make the rest up as I go along. I only
have to stop Chloe being friends with Zuzanna for
one week till the school trip. How hard can it be?

CHAPTER SIX

Worksheets and Wishes

Wednesday afternoon

At lunchtime I make a start on showing Chloe around again but it is not easy. Everyone has gone Chloe Clarke mad. I can't really understand it – just because she's pretty and cool and rich and new. I remember when being new used to be hard work.

I was new once. I didn't come to this school till

51

Year Two. This was because my mum and dad were being completely fussy and decided that we simply had to move house because they were bored with the old one.

I can remember walking in and looking at all the faces staring at me and saying, "Muuuuuuuum!"

Of course my mum was completely unsympathetic and said, "Don't worry, Emily, you'll soon settle in. Next week you won't even remember you're new."

What parents don't understand is that when you change school, you are new for about two or three years. And even then you only stop being new if some even newer people come along and take over your newness. If nobody new comes along to take over you can probably be new for ever. Well that's how it normally is, but Chloe doesn't seem to be having a problem.

I am exhausted with trying to keep her occupied and out of Zuzanna's way. Everywhere I take her Zuzanna seems to spring up saying, "Hi, Chloe, wanna come and look at my boy band pictures?" or, "I've got a new strawberry gel pen, do you want to smell?" and I have to say, "Sorry, Zuzanna, we are working to a timetable," and drag Chloe away. I don't know if I can keep this up until the school trip.

Mrs Lovetofts gets very excited this afternoon as she has come up with a "fabulous living history" type homework. "What I want you to do, class, is to walk around our local town . . ." she raises her eyebrows and gives us a little smile as if going into the town might actually be rather wicked – I think she has had quite a sheltered life, ". . . and look at the buildings."

I'm hoping there's more to this because so far it does seem a little bit dull.

"There is one very famous Tudor building in the middle of town and I want you to identify it and write about it. I would also like you to illustrate your project. Now, because this is quite a difficult assignment, I am giving you till next Monday to complete it. You can work in pairs if you like," she adds.

Why do teachers have such a thing about working in pairs? I have no idea what a Tudor building looks like anyway. If Bella were here she'd know – Bella always knows everything. I flick Wavey Cat's paw. I wish Mrs Lovetofts would give us a worksheet or something. They always make things easier.

"Here is a worksheet," Mrs Lovetofts says.

Oh no! That was probably my one moment in time for my wish to come true and I used it up on a worksheet. Now I'll never get Bella to come back! She'll live in Wales for ever with her goats and New Emily and I'll be stuck with no one except a burping boy and a Wavey Cat which grants all the wrong wishes!

When I get out of school Gran is waiting by the gate to drive me home. You might think that is a good thing, but you would only think that if you had never been in a car driven by my gran. Still, it does at least give us a chance to discuss the baby name situation, though I'll wait till we get home. I don't like to speak while Gran is actually driving; she needs all her concentration facing forward. Also she swears a lot at other drivers so it is best to pretend you are finding the scenery really interesting.

We make it home in one piece, though judging from the swearing we had a few near misses. I ask Gran what will happen if Mum and Dad don't get round to naming the baby.

Gran says, "Well I expect they will be arrested and it will be in all the papers. But don't worry. They'd have to go to court first and they don't have any room left in the prisons anyway so judges are always trying to let people off."

It is all very well for Gran to say "don't worry"; she is already an orphan and has had years to get used to it. I have never been parentless (although thinking about it I might not notice that much difference at the moment). I suppose I could go to court and beg for mercy.

I can hear the judge saying, "Mr and Mrs Sparkes, you have been completely useless as parents but I will give you one last chance. Name your child now!" And Dad would be desperate to save Mum from prison and blurt out the first thing he saw and for ever after I would have a sister called Wig. Either way it's not good.

Gran comes in to see Mum so I give up any hope of getting food or motherly care of any sort because they will spend the next two hours nattering about baby stuff and drinking tea. I am wandering about a bit trying to think of something to do that does not mean using a lot of brain power as mine is worn out from school when I suddenly remember I haven't checked my advent calendar today. So I do and it is exactly ninety-nine days till Christmas.

I always start my advent calendar countdown early – luckily the supermarkets start Christmas in September to cater for very organised people like me. I bought five calendars which means I can have a chocolate every day till Christmas and I always know exactly how many shopping days are left. Most people don't start till the beginning of December and then they wonder why they get in a last-minute panic. I go to tell Mum and Gran the good news about it being only ninety-nine days but they don't seem as excited as me.

At least the computer is working again so at least I do get to chat to Bella.

Bella says: Wales is sooooo
great - we have been pony
trekking! My pony was called
Penny.

 Emily says: Sooooooo totally
jealous. Here is totally awful.
Mrs Lovetofts is trying to make
me partners with Gross-Out for
the school trip.

 Bella says: Noooooooooooooooo!

 Emily says: Yes! And last night
I had to have a lift home in
his van!

 Bella says: Noooooooooooooooo!

 Emily says: Yes. And also we
have a new girl called Chloe.
She is in your chair.

Bella says:Noooooooooooooooo!

The conversation is getting a bit boring so I decide to change the subject.

 Emily says: What about you?

 Bella says: I am going to New Emily's for tea tomorrow so won't be online.

 Emily says: Noooooooooooooooo!

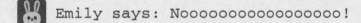 Bella says: Here is a cute picture of a cute pony to cheer u up.

 Emily says: Oh sooooooo cuuuuuuute!!!! You are totally my BFF!

 Bella says: U 2. Why do u keep saying totally??

CHAPTER SEVEN

The Endship Sea

Thursday morning

Dad is taking me to school again this morning. He is very cheerful. I tell him about Bella's pony trek and he says, "Bella's mission to boldly go where no girl has gone before. Wales!" Then he says, "Do you get it? Pony trek – *Star Trek*?" I tell him that *Star Trek* is for old people but he is still cheerful. He never used to enjoy going to work so much.

As we are pulling up outside the gates I see Chloe Clarke being dropped off in a great big white four-by-four car. I wait till she goes in before getting out of Dad's van.

As I am getting out I say, "Do not even think of getting Gran to pick me up tonight."

He says, "Oh, err . . . hmmm. We haven't thought about that, have we?"

I don't know who "we" is. Surely he's not expecting me to make my own transport arrangements on top of everything else.

Then he says, "Don't worry. I'll get *someone* to come."

So I am abandoned at the school gates in the hope that one day *someone* might remember to pick me up. I don't think my parents have any understanding of the importance of a good start to the learning day.

When I get in, Zuzanna has already got Chloe over by her chair and is showing off her drinks bottle with the "flippy-uppy" lid. This is another area in which I can't compete. All the girls in our class have cool drinks bottles with a picture of a *sooooo cuuute* kitten or a special bit that you can put in the freezer or a flippy-uppy lid. I have a plastic bottle that used to have spring water but now has tap water and a peeled-off label. My old water bottle broke after I chewed the top. I don't think they are very well made to be honest – they should be made out of some super-strong plastic that can stand up to a bit of chewing. And of course Mum won't buy me a new one now because she says it's a waste of money and I should be pleased to use an old plastic bottle because it shows I am good at recycling. Somehow I don't think that's going to impress Chloe much.

Luckily at break Mrs Lovetofts gives me and Chloe the job of staying in and getting all the little bits of Blu-tack off the walls. This is a bit boring but at least Zuzanna is out of the way. Though she keeps pacing up and down past the window, looking cross and trying to see what is going on. What is actually going on is I am climbing on the tables trying to reach bits of stuff stuck up on the walls, and Chloe is standing around being the holder of the Blu-tack ball because climbing is *not really her thing*. I see Zuzanna is coming past again and I think I had better sort out this partners thing.

"You know the Tudor Times Time-Travel Trip?" I say. "Do you want to be partners?"

"Oh, not you as well!" Chloe says. "Zuzanna's already asked me – sometimes it's not easy being so popular."

I can't believe it! Zuzanna has asked her already. I wonder when she managed to sneak that in – probably while I was hiding my water bottle.

Across the playground I can see Gross-Out chasing Gracie McKenzie with something on the end of a stick. He does it to all the girls – he says it's dog poo but it's probably just mud. The thing is it's not easy to check when you're running for your life.

"So are you going with Zuzanna then?" I say with a horrible sinking feeling.

"Weeell. I haven't made my mind up yet," she says. "I'm just waiting to see which one of you I like best."

"Oh. OK," I say, trying to sound understanding, which is not easy as I don't see why anyone would like Zuzanna.

"Tell you what though, I'll do the Tudor building homework with you."

"Oh. Cool!"

"We can meet in town."

"What? On our own?" I say quickly and then wish I hadn't.

"Oh, don't tell me you're not allowed into town on your own either. That's exactly what Zuzanna said. What is it with this school?"

"Of course I'm *allowed*," I say. "I'm always going on my own."

"Good, because I don't really know my way around and Zuzanna's only allowed in town if her mum comes too, which is totally *dullsville*."

"Yeah. Dullsville. Totally," I say. I have never been allowed to go around town on my own either but I will have to work something out.

"Cool. Saturday morning then?"

"Great," I say.

And with that the bell goes and everyone comes piling back in and Joshua Radcliffe is so busy smiling at Chloe that he bashes into the table and nearly knocks me out of the window.

After break we have to do pretending we are in Tudor times and writing what it's like to be either rich or poor. I don't really see what the point of it is unless you are actually intending to become a Tudor one day. Chloe starts writing straight away. She has big, roundy handwriting and instead of dots over her "i"s she does teeny little hearts. If Bella saw that writing she would roll her eyes and say, "Purleeze!" Bella does not like girly things. But it doesn't matter, I can put up with any amount of girly if it saves me from a Gross-Out worse than death. I can't think what to write so I lean over and ask Chloe, "Are you doing rich or poor?"

"Rich of course," she says. She lets me read her writing which is all about being very rich and having servants and getting them to make you pizza or ice cream whenever you want.

"I don't think they had pizza in Tudor times," I say.

Chloe gives me one of her *you are a saddo* looks and then writes:

Of course there was no such thing as pizza in Tudor times but if I was rich I would make my servant invent it.

She looks at me and says, "I know all about servants you see, because we've got one."

"You've got a servant?" I say.

"Yes."

I just say, "Oh," because I've never been in a situation where you have to talk about someone's servant.

"She picks me up from school," Chloe says, "in my parents' four-by-four of course – we don't give our servants their own cars."

I think it's safest to just say, "Oh," again.

"How do you get home?" asks Chloe.

"Err. It depends," I say. "Better get on with this writing."

I start:

I am a very rich Tudor girl who has everything she could wish for, except for a mother's love.

My story is going to be about Emmabella, who has her own pony (called Penny) and loads of clothes and stuff but since the birth of her new baby sister her mother has stopped caring for her altogether. I am just getting to the interesting bit where Emmabella is being scolded by her mother for bringing her pony indoors, when she only wanted someone to talk to, when suddenly it is lunchtime.

I haven't had a chance to make a Zuzanna avoiding plan as I've been working very hard on my *creativityness*, and I have to think on my feet. So when Zuzanna and Nicole and Babette come rushing over I link my arm through Chloe's and steer her over to the warm lunch boxes saying, "Come on. I've got something to show you." I am going to take her to the ENDSHIP SEA.

The ENDSHIP SEA is a bench in the playground. It is called the ENDSHIP SEA because it has "ENDSHIP SEA" spelled out in plastic letters along the back. For a long time I thought the ENDSHIP SEA was something to do with pirates. When we were young Bella and I used to sit on it and pretend we were sailing the seven seas in search of treasure. In the end we found out it was supposed to say "FRIENDSHIP SEAT" but the F, R, I and T fell off. Still, it was mine and Bella's favourite place to sit and watch everyone else rushing around (sometimes we still pretended we were pirates, even in Year Five, but don't tell anyone).

Chloe does not look as impressed as I'd hoped with the ENDSHIP SEA but she sits down anyway. It is a bit miserable and grey outside but at least it is quieter away from the Chloe Clarke Fan Club.

"So why did you come to this school?" I ask. "Why didn't you stay at Magnolia Hall?"

"Weeell," Chloe says in her funny accent, "my

mum thought it would do me good to experience life in an ordinary school. Just for a bit though – I'll be going back soon."

"Not before next week though?" I say, suddenly getting worried.

"No, I don't think so. My mum's still working on it," she says with a smile.

I open my packed lunch which is some leftover pizza, a hard-boiled egg, carrot sticks and an apple. I take out the apple and shut the lid quickly. How can you hold your head up and eat cold pizza and hard-boiled eggs with dignity? I don't understand how my mum's brain works when it comes to packed lunches. I mean you'd never eat that at home, would you? Imagine if you got your dinner one night and it was cold pizza, a hard-boiled egg and a pile of carrot sticks. I can just imagine my dad's reaction if he got that. My dad doesn't think anything is dinner unless it's got gravy on it. My mum wants us to be vegetarian but she hasn't got the energy to explain it all to my dad.

Chloe's lunch looks much better. She has white bread and jam (although it is probably specially selected jam made from really posh organic strawberries), crisps, a chocolate bar and *no* fruit. A proper lunch.

"Do you want to go back to Magnolia Hall then?" I ask. I don't feel comfortable calling it Mag Hall like Chloe – I think you have to be rich to call it that.

"Of course," Chloe says. "I am not staying in this dump."

I do not like anyone calling my school a dump especially when they are sitting on the ENDSHIP SEA.

"It's not that bad," I say, looking about to try to find some good bits.

"Maybe not to you," Chloe says, "but at Mag

Hall we have really modern stuff, like a swimming pool – not that I need one of course because we've got one at home – and they have shiny tables and chairs and loads of computers and a fountain in the grounds and, and ..." she looks around her, "... benches with proper signs on. Come on," she says. "Let's go in, I'm freezing."

As we step into the classroom, Chloe is immediately snatched up by Zuzanna who wants to show her a magazine about the NV Boyz. They are a boy band who everyone says will win *The X Factor.* (Except my gran. She wants Brenda Belter to win because she sings songs from ancient times when my gran was young.)

"Where have you been, Chloe?" Zuzanna says. "We always have lunch in here." Zuzanna and Chloe walk off arm in arm giggling and I am left standing on my own. It's times like this when you really need your best friend not to be boldly going through Wales.

CHAPTER EIGHT

Aliens, Llamas and Bearded Ladies

More Thursday

In the afternoon we have to draw a picture to go with our Tudor writing. I am not very good at Art – well, I am OK at some bits – but I am definitely mostly hopeless at drawing people. All my people look like aliens. It's probably my dad's fault, exposing me to so much *Star Wars* and *Star Trek*. Pretty much everyone I draw looks like an alien, except if I try to draw an actual alien, they tend to look more like scarecrows.

Chloe is doing a lovely picture of a girl with a lacy dress and ringlets shouting at servants. I draw Emmabella standing next  to her pony. Emmabella doesn't turn out too badly, except that her lacy collar looks a bit like a beard – but the pony definitely doesn't look right. I am just hoping no one will really notice when Chloe leans over and says, "Your girl looks like Noah and your pony looks like a llama."

Which cheers me up really, because at least it is a step up from aliens.

"As I have my own pony, I know exactly what

they look like," she says, "and it's definitely not like that."

I have a bit of a think until I get a good idea. I go through my story and change it so Emmabella is an unfortunate bearded girl and her only friend in the world is a llama (called Penny). I think this will be fine. The Tudors loved freaky people and strange animals. Anyway it is just in time as Mrs Lovetofts is collecting up the books.

Then she suddenly says, "Oh no! I haven't thought of any homework again!" She glances worriedly in the direction of Mr Meakin's office as if she's trying to decide what to do and says, "Homework for tonight will be to make a cover for your rough work books!" and she gives out the rough work books and mutters about headaches again.

Chloe nudges me and says, "Give me your mobile number, Emily."

"Oh," I say. "Why?"

"Because we need to arrange to meet up in town and, like, we *are* supposed to be friends," she says, giving me the *saddo* look. It's a funny sort of friends, I think, not at all like me-and-Bella friends, but it will do for now. And I am very pleased that Zuzanna overhears and is scowling.

"You have got a mobile, haven't you?" Chloe says suspiciously, as if there is a lot riding on the answer.

"Oh yes," I say. "Totally."

You are probably surprised that I have got a mobile when my parents can't even provide me with the basics like a decent school water bottle, but it is only my dad's old one which is really big and yellow and far too embarrassing to

78

actually take anywhere. I only use it in the house so really it's a non-mobile mobile. But at least I've got a number and I quickly scribble it down on a piece of paper whilst Mrs Lovetofts drones on about homework.

I am about to go out of school when I remember there is no one to take me home. Given the awful experiences of the last week, this doesn't seem like such a bad thing and I am just thinking it will be very nice to actually walk home by myself when Zuzanna's mum comes bursting in.

"Emily, sweetheart," she says. "You're coming with us."

"No. I—"

"Yes, Emily," Mrs Lovetofts says. "Your mum has just phoned. Mrs Kowalski is dropping you home."

Do they do it on purpose, do you think? I mean, do you think my parents have a list of the Top Ten Worst Journeys Home from School? I wonder who it will be tomorrow. I suppose I should be glad that Daleks can't drive.

Zuzanna's mum is already chattering away to Mrs Lovetofts about the Tudor Times Time-Travel Trip. She is one of those mums who is always at school so she knows everyone. She comes on all the school trips and always dresses up. When we did Victorian Times she wore a really tight lace-up top and kept saying, "I'm just a serving wench," till Mrs Lovetofts told her she'd got the wrong century and gave her a brown shawl. She always helps at the school fete and disco (last time she wore an Abba blue shiny jumpsuit) and last year she was Santa's fairy helper at the Christmas bazaar (she didn't really look right because she was bigger than Santa, even with a pillow stuffed up his coat).

The journey home is not good. Luckily Zuzanna sits in the front and I go in the back so we don't have to talk to each other, but her mum can't stop talking.

"How's your poor mum getting along having a new baby at her age?" she says.

"Fine," I say, though I don't really understand what she means by "at her age" – it's not like she could do it at someone else's age, is it?

"Oooh. I must come round for a natter. Zuzanna can come round too. You'd love to see the baby, wouldn't you?"

Zuzanna makes a grunty noise.

"What's the baby called?" says her mum.

Fortunately we pull up outside my house before I have to answer and I grab my stuff to get out.

"I'll just pop in and say hello," Zuzanna's mum says. What she means is she wants an excuse to stand around talking for an hour, which means I'll never get any tea.

"Mum's in bed," I say quickly.

"In bed?"

"Yes. She gets tired."

"Oh dear," Zuzanna's mum says. "It is hard for *older* mums."

Oh. Now I get it. It is very embarrassing when other people notice that your mum is far too old to have babies. Gran did warn her that would happen.

When I get in I go dashing upstairs to see Mum. She is not in bed, she is standing by the changing unit where baby Yoda is screaming, quite amazingly loudly. I tell her I am not going in anyone else's car again. So far this week I have had a lift with:

Monday: Mrs Lovetofts (so I had to stay at school for an extra forty minutes and then talk about Tudors all the way home)

Tuesday: Gavin's mum (oh, the shame!)

Wednesday: Gran (oh, the near-death experience!)

Thursday: Zuzanna (oh, someone give me a break!)

It is turning the end of the school day into a highly stressful experience which can't be good for me. Mum sticks her head up and says I will "flipping well have to get used to being highly stressed like the rest of the family" but I think I caught her at a bad moment judging by the smell and the enormous baby wipe mountain she seems to be building up.

When she has finally wrestled baby Yoda back into her sleep suit (I think it is sensible not to point out that she has done the poppers up wrong), she makes a real effort and says, "So. How was school?"

I am pretty sure she is not actually interested and I test her out by saying, "Fine. We had crocodile soup for lunch and then Mr Meakin sacked all the teachers.'

She says, "That's nice," and starts clearing up all the baby wipes so I know I am right.

I bet when Chloe Clarke gets home the servant opens the front door for her and then she goes to sit with her mama in the drawing room while the maid brings tea. I'd settle for a quick hello and a bag of crisps to be honest.

CHAPTER NINE

Baby Blues

Even more Thursday

It is six days since Mum got out of hospital. You would think that by now she would have at least managed to tidy up the living room. And I think she's forgotten that we have a Hoover. Soon we could be living in unsanitary conditions, like the Tudors. We might get plague. Mrs Lovetofts would probably come round and make notes. Plague is really her thing at the moment.

Mum does not seem to have noticed the potential for sickness and death, however. Other Emily B. says she's probably got baby blues. Her mum works in a chemist's so she should know. The signs to watch out for are if she starts eating lots of chocolate biscuits and watching *Jeremy Kyle* instead of loading the dishwasher. Anyway, Other Emily B. said her mum's going to phone up my mum for a natter later and she'll be able to tell my mum all about being depressed, so that should cheer her up.

At six o'clock I go to meet Bella in computer space.

Emily says: How is Wales today?

There's no reply. Then I remember – Bella has gone to New Emily's house. I send her a message anyway.

Emily says: Hope you had a
nice time with New Emily.

(This is not true. I hope she had a totally
horrible time and has decided that she hates New
Emily, and all Welsh people and Wales, but that is
not the sort of thing you put in messages.)

 Emily says: Mum says you can
move back and live with us if
u want.

(Mum didn't really say this, but then again she
probably wouldn't notice if Bella moved in. I don't
think we'd get away with the goats though – well,
maybe one or two.)

 Emily says: Chloe is still
sitting next to me - she is
trying to be my best friend

but I don't really like her.
You are my BFF of course.

Suddenly from under a pile of paper next to the computer there is a bleeping sound. I scrabble about a bit and find my big yellow phone. I have a text!

Hi, Emily. It's Chloe.

Chloe! I am a bit in shock but I am still quick-thinking enough to go into the other room – in case Chloe has some sort of special-vision phone that can read messages from the computer. Rich people have loads of stuff like that.

Chloe! Hi!

R u doin book cover homework?

Soon.

What r u gonna do?

Stick on pictures I think.

I haven't got any pictures.

I could send her some pictures I suppose. I don't think Bella would mind.

If u text your email I can send u some soooooo cuuuuuuute animals piccies – if u like.

OK. But I expect mine will be better than yours cos Art is totally my thing and definitely not yours.

I know.

89

Spose u might be good at something else but u haven't found out what it is yet.

This sort of thing always worries me. Like what if the one thing I'm really good at is building igloos or painting white lines on the road or training camels? What if I am such a natural with camels that they'd call me the "Camel Whisperer" and my fame would be known across the deserts of the world? How would I ever know? I could waste my whole life being a teacher or a doctor while the camels of the world run wild.

Chloe texts me her email address and I send her Bella's cute animal pictures. Now I am sending them, I wish I hadn't said I would because really they are just mine and Bella's to share, but it's too late now.

Before I even have a chance to start concentrating on thinking about starting my homework, the phone rings. After about six rings I realise that, as usual, no one is going to answer it so I stick out my hand and pick it up. It's Other Emily B.'s mum.

My mum is upstairs, of course, so I have to run all the way up. I say, "It's Other Emily B.'s mum."

Mum says, "What the heck does she want?"

It is a very good job I have lived with my mum for eleven years and I know what she's like. I always press the phone against my shoulder when I tell her who it is, otherwise she would have no friends at all.

Mum waves her hand in the direction of the bed and says, "You'll have to look after, umm, thingy."

Perhaps she's finally starting to notice how inconvenient it is for Yoda not to have a name. I will tell Gran later and she will be pleased there is some progress.

Mum takes the phone and says, "Francesca! How lovely," while pulling a face which means it's not lovely at all. It is a good job our family is too old-fashioned to use Skype.

I am left in charge of Yoda. This is quite easy

because she just lies on the bed looking surprised. I don't know if she is surprised that I am looking after her or if she has just thought of something she hadn't thought of before. Like when you suddenly think, *I wonder what an apple tastes like with tomato sauce on?* or something. It's that sort of face. Although when you come to think of it I suppose if you're only seven days old everything you think of is something you haven't thought of before:

A list of things babies might think of:
What is that square, bright thing?
Answer: A window.

Who's that scruffy, hairy man?
Answer: Your dad. He doesn't always look like that - only when he's having

"sleep deprivation". Mind you, don't get your hopes up, he is one of the scruffiest dads at school even on normal days. (Not as bad as Amy-Lee Langer's though, but he's got an excuse - he's been in prison.)

When can I have some proper food? Answer: When you get some proper teeth of course - or you'll just have to sit there looking at it. (I don't know why they don't give babies false teeth - then they could eat properly straight away. I might invent them.)

Who's going to win The X Factor? (That last one is a joke - it's going to be a few months before she gets round to thinking about that, though I think it's going to be the NV Boyz.)

Mum is off the phone and laughing.

"Ha! That Francesca Bunter is a funny woman! Do I look like someone with the baby blues?" Then she looks in the mirror and bursts into tears.

CHAPTER TEN

A Bit of Dinner Would Be Nice

<u>Still</u> Thursday! Seriously.

I am not really sure what a person with the baby blues is supposed to look like but if it is someone with baby sick and chocolate down their nightie and mad fuzzy hair held back with a cereal packet clip then I think maybe Mum looks about right. I am very good though and jump up and put my arm around Mum.

"You look fine, Mum," I say, which is actually a white lie, so it doesn't count. "And you're not depressed, you're just grumpy." (As I am being very nice I don't say "as usual" out loud, I just think it.)

Mum wipes her nose on her sleeve and stops blubbing. She gives me a little smile.

"It's just because I'm not getting much sleep," she says. "I think I'll go and have a shower as you're doing such a good job looking after, err . . . "

"It's OK, Mum. We'll be fine."

Me and Yoda lie on the bed and I tell her about her family.

"Don't worry about Mum crying, she's always bursting into tears about something or other. Films, music on the radio, books. Once she even cried when she accidentally stood on a ladybird. Gran says she's been overly emotional her whole life. You'll get used to it and she's not as sensitive as Daniel Waller."

Yoda seems to be thinking about that one. She

is pulling a thinking face. Or she might just have wind.

"You have one really nice sister, that's me. You don't have any other brothers and sisters because Mum was spending ages trying to have a career. Then she got one and decided she didn't want it and had you instead. Gran had something to say about that as well."

We don't get any further because Mum is out of the shower and has even washed her hair. She picks up Yoda and we all go downstairs. She must be over her baby blues for a bit (but I've hidden the TV remote and eaten all the chocolate biscuits just in case).

I am just thinking about considering starting my homework *again* when Dad gets home. He makes Mum a cup of tea and says she looks tired, which makes Mum cry again.

I say, "She looks much better than she did half an hour ago." Then Dad tells me off for being rude when he's the one who brought the whole thing up in the first place. Dad says he's going to get fish and chips for dinner to save cooking. I am very glad about this because recently I have had for dinner:

Sunday: Some toast and an apple because Dad forgot to go shopping.

Monday: Gran's "mystery ingredients" casserole heated up in microwave. Scary!

Tuesday: Almost nothing because Mum and Dad fell asleep and then beans on toast at 9.07 p.m. when I managed to wake Dad up.

Wednesday: Dad's special baked potatoes with baked beans and Cheese - NOT. (That's what he said he was making - but there were no potatoes and no cheese left so just beans on toast again actually)

Mum is in a bit of a difficult place with the fish and chips. She doesn't really approve of takeaways; on the other hand she has now failed to provide for her family for nearly a whole week so she can hardly be surprised if we take matters into our own hands.

"I suppose chips are fine this once," she says. "But we are going for healthy eating from tomorrow." Dad rolls his eyes at me. Healthy eating definitely doesn't include gravy.

Then Mum says, "Soon we are going to start growing our own vegetables too, so that they will have no carbon miles."

"I have to do three times as many carbon miles going to work to pay for all this green stuff," Dad says, which is pretty brave of him.

Mum takes a deep breath in through her nose and says, "Perhaps you would like me to forget about maternity leave altogether and have the baby in a sling round my neck at the office."

Dad goes off quick to get the fish and chips. He knows when he's beaten.

After the fish and chips (of which I get nearly all chips and hardly any fish because Mum said she didn't want a whole piece and would share with me but then she forgot and nearly finished it), I finally get around to starting my homework. I print off pictures of the cute animals that Bella has sent me. Then, because I totally need a break from creativityness, I decide to check my advent calendar again. It is now only ninety-eight days till Christmas. I only just slightly mention this to Mum as she is draping wet nappies over the radiators (she is using cloth ones, for the environment – she's doing very well at "using them" but not so well on the "getting them washed and dried" side of things) and she starts ranting again.

"Shopping days! Christmas should be a peaceful family celebration, not all about shopping." This is completely a bad start and I am just thinking I need to change the subject quick because she is on an "eco-roll" when it is too late and she says the terrible words.

"This year we are going to have a simple Christmas. I am going to give people *home-made presents.*"

Now if there's one thing I'm sure of, *home-made* and *presents* do not go together. I do not want a knitted bobble hat and some flapjack wrapped in cellophane. I talk to Dad about it as I'm sure he doesn't want home-made presents either. In fact I know he doesn't, he wants a *Star Trek* box set – he's been going on about it for ages. Although there's no point really, because Mum will never let him watch it.

"Home-made presents alert, Dad!" I say.

But he just says, "Christmas? That's not for ages." This must be what Mum always says about him failing to plan ahead. Ninety-eight days can just whizz by if you haven't got yourself organised.

I think my mum has got herself in a big muddle – presents should be bought from shops and dinner should be home-made, not the other way around!

This is very concerning. To make myself feel better I decide to have another check in my advent calendar for any chocolates I have missed so far. It is always worth triple-checking in case you actually forgot to open a door one morning and then had memory loss – which you didn't remember – and a chocolate has been sat there for ages. Sadly, I don't seem to have suffered from memory loss this week. However, while I am checking I have the most brilliant *brainwavey* idea for my book cover. Chloe is going to be so impressed.

CHAPTER ELEVEN

The Great Tudor Bake Off

Friday, finally!

Thankfully Dad gets a half day on Fridays so he can drop me off and pick me up. I don't think I could take another humiliating experience this week. Chloe is already in and showing everyone her rough book. She has covered it with pictures of the soooooo cuuuuuute animals. She has cut them all into heart shapes outlined in silver pen.

It looks really good, except she has had to sacrifice the bunny's ears for the sake of symmetry.

"Let's see yours then," she says.

I have made a rough book advent calendar! It is only five days long though. One door for every day, Monday to Friday.

Instructions for Rough Book Advent Calendar
(Copyright E. Sparkes. Patent pending)
Materials:
One piece of thin card

(I used a cereal box – I couldn't find an empty one so there was a slight cornflakes spillage problem.)

Some pictures

(Five actually – unless you live in a country where they go to school on Saturdays, in which case you need to forget this and put all your efforts into getting your parents to move.)

Wrapping paper
glue
Method:
Draw around your book cover on to the card. Cut it out.

(The card, not your book, or it will have turned into a disaster already.)

Cover the card with wrapping paper and stick it on with glue.
Cut out five little doors in the card.

This bit is really tricky and you will probably stab yourself in the hand trying to get the scissors through. You might want to ask a grown up to help you, but that would be a no-hoper if you were in my house (not that you would be, unless you have come round for tea, but there's no way I'm asking anyone round until my mum tidies up at least one room). I didn't stab myself much but I have made a massive scratch on the dining table, although there's so much junk on it no one is going to notice for at least three years and then I can blame Yoda.

Stick the card on the front of your book.

Be very careful not to stick the doors shut or it will have all been completely pointless.

Stick a little picture behind each door.

Peasy!
    I have written:

Monday, Tuesday, Wednesday, Thursday, Friday

on the doors, but you can do it in any language, even Welsh if you have to. Under each one I have put a picture of a *soooooo cuuuuuute*  animal. I tried to get pictures of cute camels as they were on my mind but there weren't any really. Much as I like camels I have to admit I haven't seen a pretty one yet – so I just did Bella's bunnies and kittens and ponies.

Chloe looks at my book and doesn't say anything for a minute.

Then I say, "Do you like it?"

"I thought you said we were just sticking pictures on," Chloe says in a definitely *not soooo cuuuuuute* voice.

"Yes, but I had a flash of creativityness."

She scrunches up her nose. "It's good but you have cheated really."

Then Gracie McKenzie comes over and says it is fantastic and I am artistically gifted.

Chloe says, "*OMG!* She is *so* not! Her people always look like aliens."

Then Zuzanna comes over and says, "Animal pictures are a bit immature, in my opinion." (She has covered her book with NV Boyz pictures.) Chloe makes a really huffy noise and Zuzanna looks at her book and quickly adds, "Unless you do them like Chloe, in hearts with silver pen – then they look really cool."

"Oh, thanks, Zuzanna!" Chloe says. "Although now you come to mention it I think you're right. Animal pictures are a bit immature."

"I've got some NV Boyz pics you can have if you like," Zuzanna says.

Chloe gives her a big grin and they go off giggling to Zuzanna's desk.

How did that happen?

At least Mrs Lovetofts likes my book cover.

She says, "Emily Sparkes, you have a highly original mind." I think this is a compliment.

This morning we are doing more Tudor stuff in preparation for our trip. Mrs Lovetofts is very pleased with herself as she has decided to do a day on Tudor food. It sounds boring but I am completely amazed to find out what Tudors ate. Loads of stuff you would think had only just been invented, like garlic and pineapples and red peppers. Mind you, that was mostly the rich people – ordinary people were stuck with boiled potatoes, cabbage and turnips.

"Henry VIII liked nothing better than a good feast," she says, "which is why I'm announcing a little class competition. I want everyone to bake a cake fit for a king! We are cheating a bit as Tudors didn't really eat a lot of cake but I'm sure good old King Henry would have loved a nice slice of Battenberg given half a chance. We will call it the Great Tudor Bake Off! Mrs Bundle the school cook will judge the best cakes on Monday afternoon and the winners will have their picture in the school newsletter."

"Isn't there a prize?" asks Chloe.

"Effort is its own reward, Chloe," says Mrs Lovetofts. No one has a clue what she means.

Mrs Lovetofts loves cake almost as much as the plague. She does lots of "bake offs". Last year she did one for the whole school and I got a "highly commended" for my "interesting buns" (which were mostly interesting because I got the cinnamon and curry powder jars mixed up, but no one seemed to notice). She has done a little pile of recipe cards. "Just some ideas here, everyone, to get your baking brains working!"

I am totally excited as I love cooking. I look through all the cards. Most people are going to  make sponge cakes but I think this sounds a bit boring. I choose Lemon and Honey Drizzle Cake and take a recipe card.

"One more thing," Mrs Lovetofts says, "as usual all cakes will be donated to the Silver Years Retirement Home, however they are requesting that we send fewer cakes than usual, as the last time we sent sixty-seven which was a little excessive, given that they have only got fifteen residents and a new 'healthy eating policy'. Because of this I suggest you bake cakes in pairs if possible."

Pairs! I grab Chloe's arm. "Do you want to be cake partners?" I say quickly. I am definitely getting in before Zuzanna this time.

She gives me a funny look and says, "I'll have to think about it. There are some concerns I have to address first."

"Concerns?"

"Yes." She picks my hand off her arm and gives it back to me. "For example, *someone* told me that you are really good friends with that ... that boy." She looks over to where Gross-Out is doing his bulging-out-eyes impression of a bullfrog (it is actually quite good especially as he has some breakfast cereal still stuck on his chin which looks just like warts).

"No!" I say quickly, knowing full well who *someone* must be. "I just had to go in his van. Once. My mum arranged it."

"Hmm. Well, I'll have to think it over," she says.

You wouldn't think she was new.

I am worrying about this all the rest of the morning and in the afternoon things get worse. Mrs Lovetofts decides that it will be a good idea to show us a programme called *Tudor Kitchen Garden*. Usually watching a film in school is OK because at least it's not actual work, but this is utterly not OK. It is the *boringest* video I have ever watched and that includes the time we had to watch *The Life Cycle of the Common Newt*. There is an old gardener and a woman and mostly they grow turnips and make a disgusting-looking soup called pottage – *all day*. Mrs Lovetofts thinks it's marvellous of course. She says "living history" so many times I think she may have got stuck in a time loop but then she breaks free and says, "Gavin would you please stop doing that to Alfie's nose."

I am just about dozing off entirely when Chloe nudges me and passes me a note. It says:

Tick True or False and return:
  I, Emily Sparkes, completely and tripley swear that:
  a) I will never set foot in Gross-Out's van again, ever.
  True
  False
  b) I will never again change homework agreements without checking.
  True
  False
  I swear this to God, the Queen and Simon Cowell.
  Signed....................(E. Sparkes)

I look at her to see if she is being serious but she is totally pretending to be engrossed in how to grow Tudor cabbages, so I tick "True" both times and sign it and slide it back over.

Chloe scribbles another note which says:

OK - you can be my cake partner.

Phew!

I am so relieved that I can't stop smiling. Mrs Lovetofts thinks it is because I am really interested in *Tudor Kitchen Garden* and gives me a merit mark.

Finally, *Tudor Kitchen Garden* is over and Chloe says, "Right then. We'll make Victoria sponge."

I say, "Oh, I was going to make lemon and honey drizzle cake."

"You can make Victoria sponge with me if you like," says a voice from behind us.

I don't know how Zuzanna manages to turn

up every time I don't want her to (which is always).

"OK," Chloe says. "I totally hate lemons."

Zuzanna gives me a smug grin but I am not giving in that easily, especially as I bet it was her who told Chloe that I had been in Gross-Out's van.

"What I mean," I say quickly, "is that I was *going* to make lemon and honey drizzle cake but Victoria sponge is a much better idea. So, so ... *Victorian*, which is basically the same as Tudor ... only later."

Chloe opens her mouth to speak but Mrs Lovetofts has arrived.

"Is there a problem, girls?" she says.

"One of us is going to be left out," Zuzanna says. "Chloe can't be partners with *both* of us." She gives me a look that is supposed to mean I have to be left out.

"Chloe and me have already decided to be partners," I say.

"Yes, but she doesn't want to make your stupid drizzly cake," Zuzanna says.

"Now then, girls, no need to get in a pickle!" Mrs Lovetofts beams. "I'll tell you what, why don't you be a three – just for making the cake."

CHAPTER TWELVE

Mum Magic

Saturday morning

My weekend has been completely taken over by homework. Chloe and I are going to Zuzanna's tomorrow. We finally managed to agree to do the cake as a three. There was a bit of a worrying moment when Chloe suggested we do it at my house. It is bad enough being poor and having no servants but if anyone sees the state of our kitchen they would probably have to inform *the authorities* (I don't really know who *the authorities* are but my gran is always informing them of stuff).

I was hoping we could go to Chloe's because I really want to see her house but she said, "Sorry, I would invite you, but we are having a swimming pool put in this weekend."

I said, "I thought you already had a swimming pool?"

She said, "A second pool."

So we agreed on Zuzanna's house. Well, Chloe sort of decided and Zuzanna had to go along with it.

Then last night Chloe texted me and said:

I hope you haven't forgotten about meeting in town. C u at 11 outside the mall.

I replied:

OK but not the mall. C u outside the library.

I hadn't forgotten about meeting Chloe. I just haven't got around to asking Mum and Dad yet. Fortunately we have to go to town anyway to buy a new baby buggy, so now I just have to persuade them to let me go off by myself for a bit.

I find it's always a better idea to tackle one parent at a time. I decide on Mum as I have some special magic words that work really well on her.

"*Mum,*" I say, "when we go into town, would it be OK if I met my friend for a bit?"

"I don't know about that," Mum says, predictably. But never fear, here comes the magic bit.

"We're going to do some *homework* (magic word one)," I say, "and we are meeting at the *library* (magic word two)."

"Oh, that's fine then," she smiles. "We'll drop you off."

See? If I'd said, "We're meeting in a café and

we're actually going to enjoy ourselves," it would have been a completely different result. My mum worries about fun.

Gran has come round to look after Yoda for the morning as we can't take her with us without a buggy and we can't go to get a buggy and leave her behind (it makes sense if you think about it long enough).

You would think that Gran coming round would mean we could get out more quickly, but Mum and Gran start talking so Dad takes his coat off again. Apparently the midwife came round yesterday (why are they called "midwives"? Is it because they're in the middle between the wife and the baby? It's the only explanation I can think of) and said Mum hasn't got baby blues but she does need to rest. Rest! If she rests any more I will have to be taken into care. Mum says she will feel a lot less blue once she has bought the Baby Eco-Jogger Deluxe.

"We could have bought one and come back by now," Dad says, but not loud enough for Mum to hear because he has already been brave once this week.

Mum goes off to get ready and Gran says, "Let's you and me go and tidy the kitchen shall we? Give your mum a hand."

It's one of those questions you can't answer truthfully by saying, "No thanks, I can't be bothered but you go ahead if you like." It's one of those things you just have to go along with. Grans are clever like that.

However, when Gran goes into the kitchen I think she nearly changes her mind. She says several swearwords which I pretend not to hear and then she starts shoving all the leftover cartons from last night's Chinese meal into a bin bag. ("This is *definitely* the last time we're having a takeaway meal," said Mum last night.)

Gran is moaning about the state of the kitchen

so much that I tell her she probably should have taught my mum to be a better housewife. This is a stupid thing to say because Gran immediately replies, "Well I'd better not make the same mistake with you then. Here, spray this inside the fridge and wipe it out." I really should have seen that coming.

Gran keeps clearing the worktop. "What are all these cornflakes doing spilled everywhere?" she says. "And the box is all ripped."

I stick my head further into the fridge.

Underneath all the rubbish she finds:

1. Tudor Times Time-Travel Trip Letter – not signed, and most likely not even read.

2. List of Baby Names – Gran is not happy about this. She magnets it to the fridge and crosses out Cheryl because she read in the paper that Cheryl said Brenda Belter was overrated. She puts down Brenda instead. I still don't think she's in with much of a chance.

3. The Must-Have Guide to Baby Buggies –
which I did last night. You would not believe
how expensive a Baby Eco-Jogger Deluxe is so I
thought Mum might want to consider something
else, especially as it is getting near to Christmas
(ninety-six days). I found all the information I
needed on a baby website (that means it was all
about babies, not just small) and I printed out a
copy of my research findings. It was actually called
"A Must-Have Guide to Baby Travel Systems"
but I think Mum and Dad would probably not
understand because they are very old sort of
parents, so I changed it to "Buggies" on their
copy. There was a picture of a really fashionable,
young mum and dad, so I left that bit off too, but
I printed out the rest:

The Must-Have Guide to Baby
~~**Travel Systems**~~ *Buggies*

Durable – Baby ~~travel systems~~ *buggies*
should be tough! Whether they are
bouncing down a country footpath
or around an airport conveyor belt,
they need to be sturdy.

(Personally I don't think it would be very safe to take a baby for a walk on an airport conveyor belt but as Mum is totally against aeroplanes for carbon miles reasons we don't need to worry.)

Flexible – Your baby ~~travel system~~ *buggy*
needs to fit in with your family
lifestyle – whether eating at your
favourite restaurant or shopping in
a boutique clothes store.

(I sometimes wonder if our family is normal.)

**Desirable – Perhaps the most
important consideration of all.
Does your baby ~~travel system~~ make** *buggy*
**heads turn? This season's colours
are fizzing orange and sherbet
yellow – take a tip from celebrity
mums and make sure your baby
~~travel system~~ says something** *buggy*
about you!

The clever bit is I added one more myself!

*Affordable - Make sure your buggy is
quite cheap. Family celebrations like
Christmas are very important and you
should make sure there is some money left
for other members of the family.*

I put the buggy guide in my bag as Mum will
clearly need to refer to it later.

Mum finally comes downstairs. I am not sure what has taken her so long because she looks more or less the same as she did when she went up there. You'd think she would be embarrassed to find her elderly mother and her child cleaning her kitchen, but she seems pleased and gives Gran a big hug, and starts crying of course. I don't get a hug. I am now apparently just expected to be a skivvy, like Cinderella only without the benefit of knowing someone with a magic wand. Finally we make it into Dad's van (not a golden carriage) and head off into town.

I am sure we are going to be late so I try to check the time on the non-mobile mobile. (Mum insisted I bring it in case of a homework-related emergency.) I have hidden it right at the bottom of my bag so Chloe doesn't see it. As I am digging around I pull out the buggy guide. "Don't forget this, Mum," I say.

Mum takes it but she doesn't bother to look at it.

"These Baby Jogger things are very expensive," Dad is saying. "You never know, we might find something just as good but a bit cheaper."

"We won't," Mum says.

CHAPTER THIRTEEN

Tudor Town Trouble – Part One

*Still Saturday morning
(though you wouldn't think it
considering the amount of
schoolwork I've got to do)*

We pull up outside the library just on time. Chloe is not there yet, just some teenager leaning against the wall.

"See you back here in an hour then," I say, slamming the door of the van.

Mum opens the window. "Don't talk to anyone," she says. Which means Chloe and I will have to use sign language. Fortunately, a bus pulls up behind and beeps its horn so they have to drive off.

I say "fortunately" because at that moment the teenager says, "Hi, Emily." And I realise it is not a teenager at all, it is Chloe. At least I think it's Chloe – it looks more like her fifteen-year-old sister, if she had one. She is wearing a huge pair of feathery earrings, skinny jeans and wedge sandals which I am not very sure are the best things for walking round Tudor Britain but we'll have to see. She is also wearing quite a lot of make-up but not actually all in the right places.

"Oh, for goodness' sake, Emily, I thought you might have made some effort!" she says, giving me her *saddo* look.

I haven't really thought much about clothes, I just have my jeans and trainers on. There is not a lot of clothing choice in our house at the moment as most of it is still living in the washing basket (and I mean *living*).

"Cool top though," she says.

I am not sure what she means – it's just a purple hoody. I look down and realise that I have splashed the stuff I used to clean the fridge all down the front. It's OK though as it seems to have made a sort of pink splatter pattern that looks quite good.

"I've brought the homework sheet," I say.

"Homework? Oh yeah. Did you bring any money?"

"Money?'

"So we can go shopping. *Duh!*"

Money is not something I ever have much of anyway. I am supposed to get pocket money but like most things it's a bit hit and miss in our house – mostly miss.

"We need to find a Tudor building," I say as I trot along beside her while she marches off towards the high street. "I've only got an hour."

"An hour! How are we supposed to go shopping in an hour?"

"But why do we need to go shopping? I thought we were doing homework."

Chloe sighs. "Because it's fun, of course."

I am getting a bit worried. It is bad enough having a whole morning taken up by cleaning the fridge and doing homework. I am not sure I can fit in fun as well.

"Perhaps we can find a Tudor shop," I say desperately.

"OK," Chloe says, "let's try this one."

She is heading into Angel's Accessories. There are lots of earrings and hair clips and handbags. None of them look at all Tudor.

"Chloe, I don't think leg warmers were invented in the fifteen hundreds," I say, finally managing to drag her back out to the street. I sneak a look at the time on the yellow phone. "We only have fifty minutes left."

Chloe sighs again. "OK. What does a Tudor building look like?"

"Well," I pull out the worksheet, "they are durable, flexible . . . fizzing orange."

"What are you going on about?"

I look down, confused, and I realise I'm looking at the buggy guide.

"Oh no! I must have given the worksheet to Mum."

"Brilliant, Emily. So you are stressing about homework we can't even do because you haven't brought the right equipment."

"But didn't you bring your worksheet?" I ask.

"No. Because I thought I was responsible for pictures. You know I'm much more artistic than you. I'll do the pictures, you do the words."

"But we need loads of words and only one picture."

"Emily. You can't hurry an artist. It will probably take me three times as long to be inspired to produce an appropriate image."

"But that's not really fai—" I start to say. Then I notice an advert in the chemist's window for mouthwash and I remember that Gross-Out's breath smells like old French cheese and I don't want to have to breathe in old French cheese for the whole of the Tudor Times Time-Travel Trip.

"OK, Chloe," I sigh.

"Good," Chloe says, "but as we don't have any idea what a Tudor building looks like we may as well just go shopping."

"Errm. I think they have black beams and white plaster," I say quickly as she takes a step towards a department store.

"Well, that sounds totally dull. They didn't have much imagination, did they? Wait a minute, look over there. The Cute Clothing Company – that shop's painted white. Definitely worth a try."

A few minutes later I am wandering around The Cute Clothing Company trying to find someone who looks as if they might know when the shop was built. So far I have seen one scary-looking goth girl who looks so miserable that I think she might be better off making wreaths with Gross-Out's mum, and a boy with really tight trousers and floppy hair. He doesn't seem to move much and I wonder if it is because his trousers are too tight or he doesn't want his hair to flop the wrong way. Either way I don't see either of them having much to say about Tudor architecture. But it doesn't matter anyway, as Chloe is already heading back out on to the street.

"Did you find anything out?" I ask, scuttling out behind her.

"Yeah, their clothes are rubbish," she says.

"I mean about the building?"

"Relax," Chloe says. "I know where there's a Tudor building."

"You do?"

"Yes. When I was coming to meet you I saw a building near the library. It was black and white and it had a plaque on it saying '1568'."

"Really? That must be the one! But why didn't you say?"

"Because it didn't sell anything interesting."

"Well let's go and have a look," I say, relieved that we might just find something to write about other than leg warmers.

"We can look on the way back," Chloe says. "I want to go in here," and she clip-clops off through a big doorway.

"Chloe, where are you going?" I try to keep up. "We're running out of time."

"We've got ages yet. Anyway, you never know, this might be a Tudor building too."

"This is the shopping mall! It was only opened a couple of years ago."

"Perhaps they took a long time building it," she says, heading up the escalator. I follow on behind gloomily.

Suddenly I hear familiar voices. "I can't understand how they can charge more for a buggy with three wheels – surely that should make it cheaper," Dad says, coming down the other escalator towards me carrying a big box. I quickly pull up my hood and hope they mistake me for a troubled teenager.

"Just try to think of it as the Starship Enterprise of buggies," I hear Mum saying as they sail past.

Fortunately the box is so big they don't notice me. It seems like Mum has got her Baby Eco-Jogger Deluxe without resorting to the buggy guide. Which is probably a good thing because if she'd read my homework sheet she might have come home with one that has black beams and a faint smell of turnips.

CHAPTER FOURTEEN

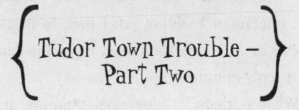

{ Tudor Town Trouble –
Part Two }

Still in town - still Saturday

I scramble off the escalator and follow Chloe into the next available clothes shop.

"Do you like this skirt?" she says, holding up a black sequinned mini.

"It's great," I say, which it is, but not very much use unless you go to a school that has a disco every week (which they probably do at Magnolia Hall).

"We might be having a little family celebration later this week," she says, quickly gathering an armful of dresses.

"Chloe, we really need to go," I say. "We haven't seen one Tudor building yet. I have to meet my parents in . . . " I sneak a look at the yellow phone, ". . . twenty minutes."

"What is that?!" Chloe says, pointing at my yellow phone which I have not managed to sneak a look at sneakily enough.

"It's . . . my phone."

"Ewwwwww!" Chloe says. "It's awful!"

"I know."

"I'm going to have to draw up another agreement for you to sign, about not carrying embarrassing accessories."

"Look, can we go?"

"Don't make so much fuss, Emily," Chloe says. "I

told you, there's a Tudor building down the road. We've got loads of time, all we need to do is look at it. How long can it take?"

Then she goes off to the changing rooms.

"Stay there," she says, pointing to a seat by the mirror. "I want to know what you think."

What I think is I have wasted the whole morning and now I'm going to have to waste most of the afternoon on the computer looking up Tudor buildings and trying to make it sound as if I actually know what one looks like.

Two minutes later she is back out in a shiny blue minidress. "Well?" she says, standing in front of me with her hand on her hip.

"It's very nice," I say.

"Nice?"

"Well – it's really short."

"Short is good, Emily," she says. She goes back behind the curtain, coming out a few minutes later in a tight purple lacy dress.

"Umm. I'm not sure," I say.

"What now?"

"Well – it's so tight."

"Oh, for goodness' sake, Emily, you're hopeless!" Chloe says. "You have the fashion sense of a, a . . . a *Tudor*!" and I am quite pleased that she has at least remembered what period of history we are doing.

Eventually she finishes all the trying on and says, "OK, I suppose we'd better go, in case you turn into a pumpkin."

"Aren't you going to buy anything?" I say.

"No, I didn't bring any money. Just trying on." She smiles.

"But what about the family celebration?"

"Oh, I've already got a new dress for that. Come on," and  she marches out of the shop. I have five minutes before my parents pick me up. My stressometer is on ten!

"Don't worry. The Tudor building is just down here somewhere," Chloe says, wandering off down the street. "There, look." She points up at a charity shop with a tatty sign above the door. "See, I told you – 1568. Now will you stop fussing?"

"Chloe, that says '156*B*' not '1568'! That's the street number!"

"Oh yes. Silly me. Hey, you're late – your mum and dad will be there by now."

"But what about the homework?" I say hopelessly.

"Oh, you'll work something out, Emily. You're good at that sort of thing, not like me." Then she adds with a smile, "Or if not, I'm sure Zuzanna will let me share hers."

I could get annoyed but the thing is she's probably right and I can't leave anything to chance. Still, I cannot believe we have spent a whole hour doing nothing. We walk quickly back to the library but luckily Mum and Dad aren't waiting yet.

"You're obsessed by homework, Emily," Chloe says, leaning against the library wall. "You need to learn to chill a bit."

She bends over to rub a speck of dirt off her wedges and I notice some words carved into a stone slab just behind her.

"Move, Chloe. Look!"

As she moves she reveals the words:

THIS LIBRARY IS HOUSED IN THE ORIGINAL
ANCIENT MEETING HOUSE. BUILT 1547.

"This is it! The library is the Tudor building. Look, black beams!"

"Oh good," Chloe says, "that sorts that out." She pulls out her mobile and takes a photo. "There. I've done the picture now so you just need to do the words."

"But that's not a picture – it's just a photo!"

"That is how I felt this building would be best

portrayed, Emily. It's art. You wouldn't understand. Gotta go. See you tomorrow."

She walks off just as Mum and Dad pull up.

"Did you get your homework done?" Mum says.

"Well. We got all the artwork done," I say as we drive off, and I think it's a pity that Mrs Lovetofts doesn't give out homework on how to say all the right things to keep people happy because then I would get an A*.

When we get home Mum and Gran immediately start nattering so I go to babysit Yoda. I don't mind actually. I think Yoda is quite cool. She listens when you talk to her and even though she can't talk back she does faces that make you think she has definitely understood. I tell her all about how much I'm missing Bella and that I have to be best friends with Chloe soon or I will end up being Gross-Out Gavin's Tudor partner and Yoda just  chews her hand and looks like she's thinking about it. I will be glad when she can talk because we will be able to discuss all sorts of things. I decide to give her talking lessons to speed things up. We make a start with:

"Mum."

"Dad."

"Emily."

And: "Can I have a fizzing orange buggy please?"

She doesn't actually say anything but she moves her mouth a lot – she is definitely working at it.

Dad leaves Mum and Gran to it in the kitchen, which is probably a good idea, and me, Dad and Yoda go to look at the new buggy. It is all in a big box and when Dad opens it there are lots of bits and instructions and pieces of polystyrene.

"It's a Baby Eco-Jogger Deluxe," Dad says, which makes him sound like he's become a bit of an expert too.

"I think we'd better wait for Mum," I say but Dad is already pushing bits together. It seems to be mostly brown and green, not even a tiny bit fizzing orange or sherbet yellow. It's a pity Mum didn't read my list – she will be sorry the next time she watches *Celeb Mom Special* (actually she never watches anything like that, mostly programmes about gardening).

When the buggy is all sorted out and Dad has put the bits he can't work out where to fit back in the box, we give Yoda a test drive. I cannot believe they have chosen such boring colours. Mum says they are "earthy", by which I suppose she means they remind her of mud, but actually Yoda does seem to like it. We push her round the living room (well, round the little bit in the middle of the living room which isn't completely covered in junk) and after only three times round she falls asleep.

When everything has calmed down a bit I go on to the computer to see if I can find anything on our Tudor library building. We have to write 250 words. As the only information I have managed to find is "The Ancient Meeting House was built in 1547", I spend the rest of the afternoon doing a lot of Emily Sparkes creativityness.

CHAPTER FIFTEEN

How Not to Make a Cake –
Part One

Sunday - homework day, <u>again</u>

Great. Dad has announced he is going to play football this morning. He has not given any thought whatsoever as to how I am supposed to get to Zuzanna's house at exactly eleven o'clock. I have tried sulking, stropping, moaning and even bursting into tears (well it seems to work for Mum) but he says he's going to get some exercise and I can get some exercise too by walking round to Zuzanna's, which "will not kill me". I tell Dad that it might actually, if a great big articulated lorry lost control and came crashing across the pavement, but he just said I'll have to take my chances and he thinks they're pretty good when walking two streets on a Sunday morning. I don't even have time to mention the possibility that I could be seriously kidnapped as he has gone out of the door, whistling.

Mum of course is no help – she will probably not even be dressed by the time I have to go, she might not even be awake. I suppose I could take her a cup of tea but she doesn't like me boiling the kettle. My parents are very confused about my personal safety. They are more worried about tea than traffic.

I am very tired myself, having stayed up late trying to think up another 242 words to go with "The Ancient Meeting House was built in 1547".

Mostly I have made a list of books that might be on the library shelves. It is not very interesting and I don't think my merit mark total will be rising, especially as Chloe emailed me her photo to stick on, which turned out a bit blurry and with half a wedge sandal in it.

I decide to get the ingredients ready for the Victoria sponge. We have divided things up – I am supposed to bring the eggs and sugar, Chloe is bringing the flour and butter and Zuzanna is providing the house which is the biggest thing so she doesn't have to bring anything else. The recipe only says two eggs but I think I will take the whole box in case of disaster. I have also got a full bag of sugar as Chloe says we are not allowed to do weighing before we get there or it won't be fair. Just as I am putting everything in a bag Mum comes in. Luckily she does not look in the bag as I know she would make me take just a couple of eggs and a little bit of sugar in a plastic pot. She is mad about not wasting food, it is part of her eco thing.

She gets really stressy if I leave any of my dinner. I told her, everyone wants to save the planet but that doesn't suddenly make you like spinach.

At twenty to eleven I set off for the journey to Zuzanna's.

Mum does not offer to walk with me or anything caring like that but, as usual, she says, "Don't talk to any strangers."

As if I'm the sort of person who wanders around saying, "Oh, hello. You're someone I've never met before. Shall we have a chat?" She makes me feel like Red Riding Hood setting off through the forest.

I am just wondering if anyone has ever seen a wolf in Aster Street when I am suddenly at Zuzanna's house, which is a bit of a surprise as it is only quarter to eleven.

Zuzanna's house is just like ours, only tidy. She doesn't have a little weedy bit of grass at the front of her house, she has a driveway with bricks in swirly patterns, and she has little trees in pots by the front door instead of a dead hanging basket. Her house also has a name: "Filipanna". It is made up of her dad's and mum's names squashed together. This makes me think her parents must be very well organised and imaginative – just think how long it would take my mum and dad to come up with a name for our house. They can't even sort out a name for their child. (Although to be fair, if they squashed their names together it would be Keithamanda, which is not very good for a house or a baby.)

I am a bit worried about being early but I don't want to risk running into any wolves by hanging about on the street too long (I know that's silly, but once you get that thought in your head ...), so I ring the bell and wait.

Zuzanna comes to the door and says, "Oh, Emily. You're early."

awesome

I say, "I know. It was a bit closer than I thought."

For a moment I think she might make me wait outside on the doorstep but she says, "Come in," in a sort of way which sounds more like, "Go away."

We go into her kitchen and her mum is there making tea. "Oh, it's just Emily," she says. "You're early."

She is wearing her glasses which are quite big and round, and I don't know why, but all the Red Riding Hood stuff is still in my head, and before I can stop myself I say, "What big eyes you've got!"

Zuzanna gives me a very funny look but luckily her mum never listens to anyone else because she's too busy talking.

"I'm quite looking forward to meeting this new young lady, Chloe," Zuzanna's mum says. "Especially as she's Zuzanna's new best friend and is going to be her Tudor day partner."

Zuzanna doesn't look at me as she is pretending to find the weighing scales but I give her the super-evils behind her back and she can probably feel it. Her mum is still going on about how she is going to be a helper on the school trip and dress as a Tudor maiden when we see Chloe's great big white car pull up outside. Zuzanna and her mum go rushing to the door and there is a lot of fussing and hello-ing – not like when I arrived at all.

"Oh, fancy your mum driving off so quickly, Chloe," Zuzanna's mum says as they all come back in. "I wanted the chance to say hello. She's the only parent in school I haven't met yet."

"Wasn't that your servant, anyway?" Zuzanna says.

"Servant?" Zuzanna's mum repeats, looking a bit surprised.

"Your house is smaller than I thought it would be," says Chloe and I see Zuzanna shoot a nervous look in her mum's direction.

"Well, it's big enough for us," Zuzanna's mum says, going a bit pink. "Now then, you girls have fun but don't make a mess." She goes off, leaving the three of us in the kitchen.

"Right," Chloe says. "We need one person to be in charge and read the recipe and two people to do the mixing and stuff. So I'll be in charge." Chloe sits up on the worktop so she can have a good view of what we're doing. "Now then," she says. "Emily. Have you got the butter?"

"You were supposed to bring the butter," I say.

"Oh, was I?" Chloe smiles. "The trouble is we're having a new kitchen fitted this weekend and I just couldn't get to the fridge."

"I thought you were having a swimming pool," Zuzanna says.

"That too," Chloe says. "Busy, busy, busy. Now, Emily, as you haven't brought any butter, we'll have to hope Zuzanna can find some."

Zuzanna finds some butter and Chloe says, "Well done, Zuzanna!" like she has done something clever, not just opened the fridge. Then we have to weigh my sugar. I am trying to pour very carefully but it keeps spilling on the floor. I am glad Mum is not there as she would already be working out how many poor people that bit would have fed for a week. When we have got two hundred and fifty grams like the recipe says, Zuzanna pours it into a big bowl.

"That's not enough!" Chloe says, peering into the bowl.

"Yes it is," Zuzanna says. "Two hundred and fifty grams – that's what you read off the recipe."

"Oh, Mrs Lovetofts is probably just trying to be healthy," Chloe says and she grabs the bag and pours more sugar in. Zuzanna tries to grab it back but Chloe snatches the bag out of the way and the rest of the sugar gets flung all over the floor.

Zuzanna tries to look at the recipe card but Chloe snatches it away. "Zuzanna, we have actually decided that I'm in charge," she says.

"But, Chloe—" I start to say, then I stop. "That's a really good idea – I like sugar."

Zuzanna gives me the super-evils for definite this time so I give her a nice smile back.

"Eggs next," Chloe says.

"I've got them," I say, getting the box out of the bag.

"Yuck!" Chloe says. "I so hate eggs."

"Really?" I say. "I like them." I clamp my mouth shut quick but it is too late because Zuzanna has already seen her opportunity.

"Oh, I'm totally with you there, Chloe. Eggs, *yeuck*!" she says, giving me a sideways grin. "But I suppose we have to have them." She picks up the egg box and then stops and stares at it. She lets out a little shriek. "Oh! These are out of date!"

I can feel my face getting hot. "What do you mean?" I say, suddenly realising exactly what she means.

"They're out of date," Zuzanna says. "Two whole days. That's so disgusting. You brought mouldy ingredients!"

My mum and her not-wasting-food obsession again. I can just imagine what she'd say: "It's only a best before date. Eggs last for ages."

"You could have killed us!" Chloe says and she and Zuzanna cling on to each other with Zuzanna making choking noises and Chloe looking at me as if I'm dangerous to know.

"My mum doesn't believe in wasting food," I say but it doesn't matter because they are not listening anyway, just hanging on to each other and saying, "Yeuck!" and, "We could have died!" and stuff like that.

Chloe is being so dramatic about pretending to be sick that she accidentally (I think) knocks the eggs off the worktop and they land on the floor in a total scrambled egg mess. Zuzanna wipes some of it up with kitchen roll but it seems to mostly spread around and mix in with the sugar from the last disaster.

When they have calmed down a bit I say, "But we still need eggs."

"No!" Chloe says. "I couldn't now. We'll have to make it without eggs. We'll have to use a bit of milk instead."

"Milk?" I say.

"But you can't make a cake without eggs," Zuzanna says.

Then we look at each other and I think we are right, but a cake is not as important as avoiding a serious *gross-tastic* incident. Zuzanna must think the same thing too because we both say at the same time, "OK, Chloe."

The cake is a total disaster. It comes out like two great big crispy biscuits which I don't think even my mum would try to make poor people eat.

"It's because there were no eggs in it," I say.

"And whose fault is that?" says Zuzanna, glaring at me.

I am just wondering if I am brave enough to point out that it might just be a tiny bit Chloe's fault when a car horn blasts outside.

"Sorry, girls. Gotta go!" Chloe says. She runs off, pushes past Zuzanna's mum who is standing in the hall and races out, slamming the front door behind her.

"Well!" Zuzanna's mum says, staring after her. She walks into the kitchen and looks around. "What on earth?!"

The floor is covered in sugar, eggs and flour. It has all sort of mixed together to make a slimy gloop and there are sticky footprints all through the kitchen and down the hall.

Zuzanna's mum does an excellent impression of an erupting volcano and Zuzanna and I have to spend the next half an hour clearing up.

It is not easy clearing up someone else's kitchen

without speaking as you can't find out where anything goes, but I think it's probably not the best time to try to start a conversation. Eventually we are finished and I put my fleece on for the walk home.

"Goodbye, Mrs Kowalski," I call. "Bye, Zuzanna." But no one replies.

We'll just have to tell Mrs Lovetofts we had a disaster.

CHAPTER SIXTEEN

Tripe and Trips

*Sunday evening and nearly
back-to-school time already*

I am very surprised when I get home because not
only is Mum still up and walking around (even
though Yoda is asleep), but she actually notices I
am a bit fed up.

"Are you all right?" she says.

What I really want to say – no, SHOUT – is, "No.

I am not all right. My best friend has gone off to be Welsh. I have absolutely no cake to show for a whole afternoon of being bossed around because of your stupid eggs and I'm probably going to end up being Tudor partners with the most disgusting boy on the planet – that's if I ever get to go on the Tudor trip because you *still* haven't read the letter!"

But what I actually say is, "Mmm," in a sort of "I suppose so," way.

That is the point where my mum is supposed to go, "Are you sure?" and come and put her arm around me and try to get me to tell her what's really the matter. But clearly my mum missed that page in the parenting manual (and a lot of other pages too) because she just says, "Oh good. Give us a hand to hang out these nappies, love."

Still at least when we have finished she makes us both a cup of tea.

"I was going to get us a choccie biscuit," she says, "but they seem to have all gone."

I decide to tell her about the cake anyway, even though she hasn't asked. "We didn't make the cake, Mum," I say. "The eggs were out of date."

"Oh, eggs don't really go out of date." (Told you.) "Never mind, I'm sure Mrs Lovetofts will understand," she says, in a way which means she doesn't actually think making cakes is very important anyway. Then Yoda wakes up and starts crying so Mum picks her up and goes and sits on the sofa to feed her.

I realise this is probably a good opportunity to talk to Mum about the Tudor Times Time-Travel Trip and to get her to sign the letter before it goes missing again. So I decide to read it out to her.

Dear parents, carers, partners of parents, and others fulfilling a similar role,
    This year we are fortunate to be able to attend Ickwell Hall for our class trip. As you know the children have been learning about

life in Tudor Britain this term. We are very
fortunate that Ickwell Hall is virtually on
our doorstep and will require only a twenty-
minute coach journey. This will be a genuine
<u>*living history*</u> *day. They will experience the*
real atmosphere of a Tudor village, meet the
residents and enjoy eating a lunch of pottage
(those with an allergy to turnips may bring
their own lunch – wrapped in a handkerchief
please).

The children will be expected to wear Tudor
costume (please see attached sheet for costume
guidance – please note trainers were not worn
in the fifteen hundreds).

The coach will leave school at <u>*8.15 a.m.*</u>
<u>*Please ensure your child is on time.*</u>
Yours faithfully,
Veronica Lovetofts
Living History Co-ordinator

"Mum? Were you listening?"

Mum seems to be drifting off into zombie-parent-land again.

"Mmm? Oh yes, yes. Tudor school trip. Fab." I wish she wouldn't say "fab" at her age.

"I need a costume," I explain as she doesn't seem to have got that bit yet. "And a note to say I'm allergic to turnips."

"You've never had any turnips."

"Exactly. So I might be allergic. It would be a very bad time to find out. Mrs Lovetofts would probably let me die to show what it was really like living without phones and ambulances."

Mum doesn't argue so I might have got away with that one. Everyone is trying to get a note. Apparently pottage is the most disgusting thing to eat in the world, and that includes celery and black olives. The vegetarians are mad because pottage is totally meat-free so they're stuck with it too. Gracie says the total point about being a vegetarian is that when there are gross school lunch things going on you get to have pizza instead. She's thinking of giving up the whole idea.

"But I really need a costume, Mum," I say.

"You had one last year."

"That was for the Victorian trip. This is Tudor."

"Oh, it's all the same. Aprons and shawls, shawls and aprons."

Then I have a brainwavey moment. I carefully balance the piece of paper showing costumes options on Yoda's head. This way Mum has to look at it.

"OK, Emily, I get the point. It's aprons and skirts," she sighs.

"It's called a 'kirtle', not a skirt. And I need a smock top."

"Yes, well," Mum says, frowning at the paper, "I think we could probably do something with an old pillowcase with some armholes cut out."

"But what about a hat?" I say. "We are supposed to have something called a 'coif'."

"Don't fuss so much, Em. We'll sort it out. We'll ask Gran."

"But even she's not that old!"

"I mean we'll ask her to make one. She's good at that sort of thing."

I go off to find a pen so Mum can sign the letter. There aren't any normal pens anywhere in our house but I find a purple gel pen.

Mum signs the letter and says, "You'd better put it in your school bag. Early start tomorrow."

Oh no! Walk-to-school day. I had forgotten.

"Can't you get your car back, Mum?" I plead. "It's very . . . *inconvenient.*"

"It will be much more inconvenient when the polar ice caps melt," Mum says. Which is clearly true but that's not going to happen tomorrow and walking to school is.

CHAPTER SEVENTEEN

How Not to Make a Cake –
Part Two

Monday

It is walk-to-school day today so, of course, it is pouring with rain. To be fair, Mum has made an effort and actually got up and dressed like a proper parent. She has also managed to find most of my school uniform and smooth it out so it almost looks like it's been ironed. Also it is very lucky that at our school at the moment there is a total craze for wearing odd socks.

Mum has worked out that we have to leave by 8.20 a.m. As it is now 8.25 a.m. and she still hasn't managed to work out how to put the rain cover on the Baby Eco-Jogger Deluxe, she is getting very stressy (think Pale Bamboo, Mum). I only happen to very slightly mention that we are going to be late and she gets quite shouty.

"Maybe you could do something to help instead of messing about on that flipping computer, Emily," she says.

Which is hardly fair when I am only Googling "Baby Eco-Jogger Deluxe" in case there are some instructions helpfully explaining how to attach a rain cover in less than fifteen minutes (and I just thought I may as well check my messages at the same time).

We finally manage to get out of the door but we are only halfway down the street when I have to come flying back to get the Tudor Times Time-Travel Trip letter. When I say *flying* I mean of course *running fast*, not that I grew wings. I am saying more and more things like that these days – it comes of spending so much time with Gran. I have noticed that old people never really say what they mean, they talk in code – a bit like teenagers, only more polite. For example, Gran never says she is going out, she always says she is *popping out*. Why *popping*? I have never seen her *pop*. Also she never has a haircut, she has a *new do*. Also, old people have totally different colours to the rest of us – my gran has things that are *mauve* and *maroon*. No one without a bus pass knows what these colours are. So she could say, "I'm just popping out to get a new do and a mauve thing," and all the other pensioners would understand her street talk and the rest of the world would be baffled. Not everyone's gran is old though; Amy-Lee Langer's gran is the same age as Mum, so I suppose all her stuff is just normal colours.

Anyway, after *flying* home and getting the Tudor Times Time-Travel Trip letter I *pop* back down the road to Mum and we finally get going. It rains the whole way and even Mum gives up pretending she's enjoying it. Gran will definitely have something to say when she hears Mum took the baby out in this weather.

In the end I just scrape into school on time, all soggy and with achy legs and not feeling at all healthy. Gross-Out Gavin and Alfie Balfour are having a "turn your eyelids inside out" competition in the cloakroom, which makes me wish I'd skipped breakfast. Then, just when I think it can't get worse, I walk into class and realise that everyone has a cake. There are cakes everywhere – some are small, some are a funny shape, some are flat and one or two even look like an actual cake. I don't know what we are going to say to Mrs Lovetofts. Perhaps we should have brought in the big crispy biscuits – at least she would have known we'd tried. Chloe and Zuzanna are already in. They are both standing around Bella's chair (I still can't think of it as Chloe's chair). As I get closer I can see there is something right in the middle of the table on a silver board, all dusted with sugar. It is a massive Victoria sponge cake. It is bigger and fatter than anyone else's in the class – it has cream and jam oozing out of the sides and looks absolutely fantastic. Chloe seems very pleased with herself.

"Brilliant, isn't it?" she says.

"It's really good, Chloe," I say and for once I am not just trying to keep her happy. "You must have been up all night making this."

Everyone is looking over at our table and saying, "Wow!" and, "Cool."

"I didn't make it, *durrrr*-brain," Chloe whispers. "I bought it this morning."

"You bought it? But why?"

"*Shhh!* We'll say we made it," she says. "We'll easily win then. Am I a genius or what?"

Zuzanna is staring at me with a very worried expression. Her plaits are definitely drooping. I wish she would say something but she seems to be waiting for me. The trouble is, I don't know what to say.

"I ... I ... well ... look, it's brilliant, Chloe, but we can't say we *made* it. I mean, it's a lie."

"And your point is?" Chloe says.

I am starting to feel a little panicky. I look at Zuzanna but she is not being at all helpful, just sort of biting her lip and looking at the floor.

Chloe says, "Don't be so *wussy*, Emily. She's not going to find out, is she? Mrs Too-Soft."

I don't like her calling Mrs Lovetofts that, she can't help being nice, but I haven't got time to fight for the rights of kind teachers now; this is turning into a bit of an emergency.

"But what if Mrs Lovetofts asks your ... your servant?" I say.

"Don't be stupid, servants aren't allowed to talk to teachers," snaps Chloe. "Anyway, we did try to make a cake. If you hadn't messed it up we'd have one. It's not fair for you to ruin mine and Zuzanna's chances just because your mum likes rotten eggs."

Zuzanna looks a bit hopeful then. Like maybe this is an excuse that works. Then she looks at me and I shake my head and she bites her lip again.

"But, Chloe, it's cheating!" I say.

Then before I can argue any more Mrs Lovetofts comes in and she is calling the register and Chloe has pushed the cake right to the front of our table and is smiling at her. Mrs Lovetofts finishes the register and beams at the class.

"My! Don't all these cakes look just fantastic?" she says. "In a little while they will all be taken into the hall and then Mrs Bundle will judge the best ones."

I am feeling more than a bit sick. Mrs Lovetofts starts to walk around the tables looking at everyone's cakes. Much too soon she gets to us.

"My goodness, girls," she says. "Well done. How super!"

"Yes," Chloe says, "we really made an effort."

I know I have almost run out of time if I am going to say something. I only have to say, "Actually, Miss, I didn't do any of it." This will not be a lie and it won't get anyone else in trouble either but then what will Chloe think? She will definitely go off with Zuzanna. She will never be my best friend. I have to decide now. I am going to do the right thing. I am not a liar. I open my mouth and say, "Actually, Miss—" and then I catch sight of Gross-Out Gavin sitting across the room taking his finger out of his nose and rubbing it on his trousers and I say, "it was really hard work."

I have done it now. I have lied to a teacher. Not just to any old teacher but to Mrs Lovetofts, the nicest teacher in the school, probably – actually, definitely – one of the nicest teachers in the whole world. I do not feel good.

"That's the best way," Mrs Lovetofts says. "Good hard work always reaps rewards, as we are going to find out next in our new topic on Tudor explorers!" and off she goes to the front of the class, smiling like she is really proud of us.

I have total worry-itus. We are bound to win the prize. Chloe's cake is the best cake I have ever seen. We will have to go up and accept an award in assembly. We will have our picture in the school newsletter. Zuzanna's mum knows we didn't make the cake and my mum knows we didn't make the cake. Some people's mums would just not worry about it, but not my mum, she'll never let me get away with it. She goes mad about lying. Even boring lying like saying you've brushed your teeth when you haven't. Imagine how mad she'll go about this one. I'll be grounded and banned from the computer for a month. Then I won't be able to chat to Bella! And I know what else she'll make me do. Go to see Mr Meakin and explain. I'll probably get excluded and everyone will hate me for being a cheat.

I cannot concentrate at all on the Spanish Armada.

For some bonkers reason known only to herself, Mrs Lovetofts gets Gross-Out and Alfie to take all the cakes through to the hall. When they get to our table Chloe says, "Be very careful with it. We put a lot of hard work into that, didn't we, Emily?"

I make a sort of noise like *munuh* which sounds a bit like *yes* and *no*, and also like I have got a mouth full of glue. Chloe doesn't seem to notice though – she beams at me, she thinks we are in this together. I suppose we are now. Alfie picks up our cake. I focus all my attention on willing him to fall over. I flick Wavey Cat's paw and secretly ask him to make Alfie have a tiny little accident. Nothing major, just to trip on a sticky-up bit of carpet or slip on a splodge of dropped buttercream and splat that cake all over the floor. Alfie falls over all the time – over his shoelaces, over his bag, over other people's bags. He has been known to fall over while standing in the dinner queue, but this time he walks calmly out of the classroom. Wavey Cat fails again. No Bella and no splatted cakes.

And so I make a decision.

I will have to do something to stop us winning by myself.

CHAPTER EIGHTEEN

Sponge Surprise!

More Monday - worst luck

At break time Chloe is soon explaining to everyone how she made the cake.

"Oh, it's not hard. At Mag Hall we had cookery lessons with Jamie Oliver. He was so disappointed when I said I was leaving. He didn't want to lose his star pupil."

"Wow," Babette says. "Can you get his autograph?"

"Of course," Chloe says and suddenly everyone is crowding round her saying, "Get one for me! Get one for me!"

While Chloe is busy I slip off to the hall. All the cakes are displayed on a long table.

There are lopsided ones, droopy ones and one that looks as though it has been dropped and scraped back up again, and there, right in the middle, is Chloe's cake, tall and golden with squishy cream and jam oozing from the sides and a delicate sprinkling of caster sugar over the top. It looks fantastic.

But not for long.

The only thing I can think to do is to squash it flat. Yes, I am going to splat that cheating cake into the Tudor era. I step up to the table, take a quick look around, breathe in deeply and raise my hand.

The door behind me squeaks. So do I. I spin round to see Zuzanna!

She is actually looking over her shoulder and doesn't notice me straight away which is very lucky as I have time to snatch my hand back quickly. When she turns round and sees me she jumps and something clatters from her hand to the floor. She swoops down to pick it up. It's very strange because it looks like the salt cellar from the teachers' lunch table, but why would she have that?

"Oh, Emily!" she says. "I . . . err . . . What are you doing in here?"

"I just came to . . . to look at the lovely cakes," I say. Lying gets easier after a while.

"Oh, me too. Me too," she says. There is a bit of an awkward pause. "Ours is bound to win, isn't it?" she says flatly.

"Bound to," I say.

She opens her mouth to say something but just then the door swings open and in comes Mrs Lovetofts, all swirly skirts and beaming smile.

"Hello, girls. Admiring your handiwork! Very well done." She leans over to get a better look at our cake. "You know," she says, "it looks almost professional."

I am having little flashes of what might have happened if Zuzanna hadn't walked in when she did. Mrs Lovetofts would have just found me elbow deep in jam and sponge. I am thinking I really need to get out of here right away-ish. And then I think that if Zuzanna is in here then Chloe is on her own and in need of a friend, and even though she has got me into a potential total baking and lying disaster, she is *still* better than being stuck with a Gross-Out worse than death. I can see Zuzanna is also thinking the same thing and we both make a dash for the door, but it is very bad luck as Mrs Lovetofts looks up from the cakes and says, "Oh, Emily. Have you brought your Tudor Times Time-Travel Trip letter in yet?"

And I have to stop and say, "Yes."

And Mrs Lovetofts says, "Good girl."

And I am just about to go again when she says, "How is Bella getting along?"

And I have to say, "Fine."

And she says, "Oh, jolly good."

And then there is one of those situations when you don't say anything but you can't actually leave.

And finally she says, "Now off you go and see your friends."

Which is what I have been trying to do for the last five minutes. I go flying (not really, see above) into the classroom just in time to see Zuzanna linking her arm through Chloe's to go out into the playground.

Disaster upon disaster! I am now completely destined to be Gross-Out's partner unless some sort of miracle occurs. I only have one day left to make Chloe my best friend but it probably won't matter as I will be kicked out of school before then anyway.

This afternoon there is assembly. Mr Meakin stands at the front of the hall and plays some classical music on a CD while everyone finds the right bit of floor to sit on. Unfortunately my bit of floor seems to be right next to Zuzanna's bit of floor. All the cakes are lined up at the front. Each one has a little slice cut out of it where Mrs Bundle has tried a bit. Chloe's cake is right in the middle. It is bigger and rounder and taller than anything else on the table. I am feeling sick.

Mr Meakin turns off the CD and clasps his hands behind his back. He does his head teacher face and everyone goes quiet.

"Today," Mr Meakin says, "I want to talk about the importance of honesty." He is looking right at me. *He can't know already!* I feel like a small slimy creature is doing forward rolls in my stomach.

Mr Meakin continues, "A lie might sometimes seem like a simple way of getting out of a problem at first, but it can soon turn into a problem in itself."

Zuzanna gives a little gasp. I am beginning to wonder if mind reading is one of the skills you need to become a head teacher. I sneak a look at Zuzanna. She is chewing her knuckles which I think means she is as worried as me, or maybe she's just hungry.

"Let's all take a few minutes to think about this," Mr Meakin says, "and to resolve to be more honest in the future." He closes his eyes and bows his head and I am suddenly very relieved to realise he is not talking about me at all. He is just doing one of those assembly talks where teachers tell children things to make them worry. It is just bad luck that he happens to be talking about honesty today, or maybe he does it a lot but I have never really taken much notice until now.

When Mr Meakin has finished making everyone feel guilty even if they haven't done anything, it is time for the cake judging.

"Everyone in Year Six has made an excellent effort,"

Mr Meakin says. "Mrs Bundle said she had a very hard time making a decision but in the end one plate stood out from all the others." Chloe is sitting at the end of the row. She is smiling so broadly you would think she was about to win the final of *MasterChef*.

"Now as you know," Mr Meakin continues, "the winner of the Great Tudor Bake Off will have their photograph taken for the school newsletter. But I am also pleased to announce that today we have a photographer from *The Evening Gazette* here." Everyone turns round to see a short man with a big camera standing at the back of the hall. "The winners will also have their photograph in the paper this weekend!"

Everyone goes "Oooh!" and "Aahh!" and Zuzanna goes "Urrgh!" and then she sort of flops over on to my shoulder.

I have never actually seen anyone faint before. There is a bit of a fuss while Mr Flint, the first aider, climbs over everyone else to get to her and accidentally makes a Year One cry by standing on his fingers. By the time he gets to us, Zuzanna has come round again but they make her go and sit on a chair at the back with her head between her knees, which looks very uncomfortable. Chloe is looking rather annoyed at the delay.

"Now," Mr Meakin says after everyone has calmed down again, "I will announce the winners." He steps over to the table. "As you can see," he says, pointing to Chloe's great big cake, "this cake made by Chloe, Emily S. and Zuzanna is excellent. Mrs Bundle wanted them to have a special mention. But she felt that another entry showed real flair by using typical Tudor flavourings – and so that honour goes to . . . Gavin and Alfie for their lemon and honey drizzle cake!"

Mr Meakin points to a flat, slightly burnt-looking cake at the edge of the table.

I cannot believe it! We didn't win. I never knew it was possible to feel so happy about being a loser.

I turn round to look at Zuzanna who is sitting up and she gives me a wobbly smile. I smile back until I remember I don't like her so I turn round again and smile at Chloe which is a bad move as she is definitely not in a smiling mood.

"It is totally unfair!" she strops as we get back to the classroom. "Mrs Lovetofts didn't tell us to use Tudor flavourings! It's just totally breaking the rules."

"But don't you think that pretending you made a cake when you didn't sort of breaks the rules as well?" I blurt out. Zuzanna looks at me in surprise. I have sort of surprised myself.

"*Urrghhh!*" Chloe says, or something that sounds like that, which means that I have definitely not said the right thing.

Alfie and Gross-Out come bursting back into the classroom shouting, "We won, we won!"

"*Urrghhh!*" Chloe says again. Luckily the bell

goes for the end of school at that moment because I can see Chloe is building up to a mega-strop.

Zuzanna looks at Gross-Out and you can see her thinking hard. Then she says, "Don't be fed up, Chloe. Why don't I ask my mum if you can come round for tea?"

"What?!" I say before I can help myself.

Zuzanna looks at me sort of sympathetically.

Chloe's face changes instantly to a smile. "Oh, thanks, *Zuzy*." (I have never heard anyone call her *that* before.) "It's so nice to have a supportive friend," she says, looking coldly in my direction. "Oooh yes. And I must make up my mind tonight about who I'm going to be school trip partners with."

Zuzanna looks at me and shrugs her shoulders. "Totally gotta go," she says and out they go together, arm in arm.

How did I let that happen? One day left and Zuzanna has completely won. I am so on my way to being Gross-Out's bus buddy.

CHAPTER NINETEEN

Gran's Garibaldis

Monday afternoon

Outside school Mum is waiting with Yoda in the Baby Eco-Jogger Deluxe. It is still raining and everyone else is running off to their nice warm cars or homes.

"Hello, love!" Mum says, in a very put on, cheery voice. "I thought we could go to Granny's on the bus. You see. Who needs a car?" She has clearly managed to blank this morning's monsoon from her mind. I think I am supposed to say something about it being a good idea, which it is clearly not, but I don't because I am in a complete worry about Chloe and Zuzanna. We start to walk down the road and I can see Chloe getting into Zuzanna's car just ahead. Then just as we are getting level and I am trying to decide whether it would be cooler to wave and say, "Have a nice time," or to totally pretend I haven't noticed them, Mum suddenly yells, "Bus!" in a screechy voice and runs off down the hill with the buggy bouncing along in front of her like she's on a supermarket trolley dash. I have no choice but to go running after her with my school bag flying out behind me. Unfortunately the bus driver is the only person for half a mile around who does not hear her shout, "Bus!" Neither does he hear her yell "Wait!" or "Stop!" apparently, because just as we get there he drives off. I also hope he cannot hear what she calls him as he pulls away or we will probably be banned from buses for life. So we have to stand in the leaky bus shelter for twenty minutes waiting for the next bus, while all the normal people with cars drive past looking like they are a bit more important than us.

I see Zuzanna's car coming with Chloe and "Zuzy" in the back. Zuzanna's mum gives me a stern look – I think she is still cross about the mess in the kitchen. I quickly bend down and pretend to look for something in my bag. A few minutes later Gross-Out's mum goes past in her van of doom. This time I make sure I am standing up and smiling, because I don't want her to think we are miserable and in need of a lift.

When the bus finally arrives it is not at all modern. It is probably nearly as old as Gross-Out's van.

"You'll have to fold that, love," the driver

 says to Mum, pointing to the Baby Eco-Jogger Deluxe. "The easy-access bus needed

a service – so it's not in service," then he looks like he's confused himself a bit and doesn't say any more.

Mum smiles. "No problem. It folds up easily with one flick of the wrist." This is what the woman in the shop told her. I could have told her it wouldn't be that easy. Sales people and adverts are only there to make you buy things, they are not meant to be taken seriously. I don't know why my mum doesn't know this yet. I learned it when I was four and my MiniChef plastic pop-up toaster refused to pop up unless you kicked it.

Mum tries a "quick flick of the wrist" several times but then remembers that she might need to press a button first. By this time everyone on the bus is glaring at us, that is: an old lady, a spotty boy with earphone thingies and another mum with a baby (who has managed to fold her buggy and store it neatly in the luggage rack and is looking a bit superior).

Mum is saying to the bus driver, "There's a button on here somewhere." He just rolls his eyes and looks at his watch. Finally, she presses the right thing and the Baby Eco-Jogger Deluxe collapses into a little heap and I think it was a very good job I reminded her to take the baby out first. When we get to sit down at last the old lady leans over and taps my mum on the shoulder.

"How old?" she says.

"Thirty-seven," Mum says.

"She means the baby, Mum," I say.

"Oh!" Mum laughs. "Don't know where my brain is at the moment. Eleven days."

"Aaawww," says the old lady – she seems to have forgiven us for the hold-up. She starts talking to Mum about when she had her baby and how it was all different then. This gives me plenty of time to sit and look out of the window and worry.

We do eventually get to Gran's but because of being late and having to get the bus back we can only stay for half an hour anyway, which suits me. Why do parents always think you should like going to your gran's house? I mean, I really like my gran, don't get me wrong. Mostly she is funny and kind and only a bit embarrassing. But going to her house is so boring. This is what happens when we go to my gran's.

Gran says, "Hello, sweetheart," and ruffles my hair. Then she says, "Cup of tea?" to Mum – and that's it. Mum and Gran start talking and totally forget I exist. If they do ever happen to notice me again they say something like:

"Awww. She must be a bit bored." (*Corrrrrrect!*) "Why don't you go and have a look at Granny's garden, sweetie?"

Garden! Why would I want to look at a garden? I am not interested in gardens.

Instead – even worse – my gran says, "I've got something for you."

This is always some sort of weird cake or biscuit

or something. I don't even know where Gran gets them from – there must be a special shop that sells stuff that only grans buy. There's no excuse for it – she's not even that ancient. She's got a laptop and everything. But when it comes to food, she's mostly prehistoric. In the last few weeks she has come up with fig rolls, liquorice allsorts and marzipan fruits, none of which you should ever even think of trying. This time it is garibaldi biscuits. If you have never had one you are lucky. They are basically loads of currants squashed inside a dried-up biscuit sandwich.

I say I don't really want one but Mum starts getting grouchy. "Granny's got them specially for you," she says, as if that's my fault. So to keep the peace I try to eat one and it is utterly horrible, which I knew it would be because it's the same every week. It's like I'm in some sort of living-child food experiment. The currants are all bitty and the biscuit stuff sticks to the roof of your mouth. I put it back down on the plate and try to get the bits off that have stuck to my teeth with my mum glaring at me like I have actually done something wrong and not nearly just poisoned myself for the sake of politeness.

I am still trying to get curranty bits out of my teeth ten minutes later when Gran says, "Have you thought of a name yet?"

"Ooh, look at the time," Mum says. "We have to get the bus."

Gran says, "I'd run you home but I'd never get that pram in my car."

"It's not a pram," Mum says. "It's a Baby Eco-Jogger Deluxe. It folds up, you know," but this time she doesn't add the bit about the flick of a wrist because I think she has had enough of that for one afternoon. "Don't worry, it's more environmentally friendly to use public transport. We're fine on the bus."

Which I am actually not, but I don't get a say in the matter. Anyway she only says it to annoy Gran because Gran doesn't believe in the environment. So off we go to the bus stop again. This time Mum folds the buggy up before the bus comes which is a far better idea and makes me wonder why anyone bothers with buggies in the first place when you could just carry the baby around in a bag or something.

It is when we are about halfway home that I see a very surprising thing. It is Chloe Clarke's house!

CHAPTER TWENTY

Result!

Later, Monday evening

I know it is Chloe's house because the gates are open and I can see her big white four-by-four car inside and no one else has a car like that. Also, it is just the sort of house that would have two swimming pools and a new kitchen and a servant. It is very big and has tall white gates and a driveway. It has loads of windows and that is all I see as the bus drives past.

"What street is this, Mum?" I say.

"Arlington Drive," she says. "Very posh." Only she doesn't say "posh" she says "poe-wsh" which is supposed to sound like a posh person talking but actually sounds like my mum has a speech problem.

That is *exactly* where Chloe said she lived. You may think this shouldn't be a surprise but the thing is, after all the fuss with the cake and everything, I was beginning to think maybe Chloe hadn't told the truth about some other stuff too, like being rich. All of which makes me even more fed up that she's gone to Zuzanna's for tea.

When we get home I am very surprised to find that Mum has tidied up a bit. It is not what you would call tidy. In fact it is probably what Zuzanna's mum would call a total disaster zone, but for us it's quite good. Mum has also managed to think of something for tea. It is only sausages, mashed potatoes and peas but at least it has three ingredients and one of them counts as a "five a day". I need this because, except for a couple of apples and some carrot sticks, I have had basically none a day for the past week, which means I now need to eat at least thirty fruit or vegetables just to break even. I have another apple while I'm waiting. Dad is very pleased to get some dinner, even if there isn't any gravy. Mum has also found a lemon meringue pie in the freezer and, although it is not quite defrosted, it is very nice and probably also counts as it is lemony so I have an extra bit to keep healthy and then go to have a think.

Thinking is not hard for me. Gran says "thinking" is my middle name but it's not, it's actually Louise (well, you weren't expecting anything too interesting, were you?), but that is just another example of pensioner street talk. It is true as you will know if you have been reading this (and have not just randomly found this page torn out and stuffed down the back of the sofa or something) that I am always thinking and not just boring stuff either. For example, I quite often think of inventions that could change the world, like a remote control to make buses arrive when you want them to or a special instant travelling machine that goes to Wales in two seconds. The trouble with being a child genius inventor is that you haven't got a laboratory to create stuff in, also no one ever listens to you long enough to realise how brilliant your inventions are. Right now though I need to think of a plan. I have one day left to make Chloe my best friend or it is: *Goodbye, dignity. Hello, life of shame.*

I am waiting to speak to Bella. She will probably know what to do – she is very good at knowing things. It is five past six and she is not online yet. I think there are two possibilities:

a) She is running late due to unforeseen events

(this is what happened to the train we took to London in the summer – unforeseen events cause a lot of problems).

b) She has forgotten.

Although I am not keen on unforeseen events, I am hoping they have occurred in Wales.

It is ten past six now. I have sent a message into the universe.

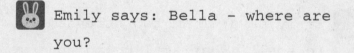

> Emily says: Bella – where are you?

But I am still waiting. And while I am waiting I am thinking. If I am trip partners with Gross-Out, everyone will think we are friends. They will think I chose to be his partner. They will think I like him. *They will think we are boyfriend and girlfriend!* It is all too awful to think about any more.

> Emily says: Bella – help!!!!!!!!

Bella says: Hi, Emily. What's up?

 Emily says: I have to totally have a new friend by tomorrow. Or my whole life is going to be ruined. It will turn into a great Gross-Out grisaster!

 Bella says: A what?

 Emily says: I am too stressed to spell. What am I going to do??????????????

 Bella says: You could try to sort things out with Zuzanna. She's quite nice you know.

 Emily says: She is sooooo not nice. She is my sworn enemy!!!! She called me a total pain and didn't invite me to her party.

Bella says: Oh yeah. Why don't you ask that new girl round for tea? New Emily's coming here tomorrow.

 Emily says: Have you seen the state of our house?

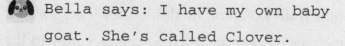 Bella says: Hey - we have goats in our kitchen but a real friend wouldn't care. Right?

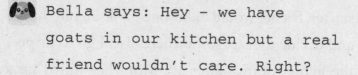 Emily says: Maybe.

 Bella says: I have my own baby goat. She's called Clover.

 Emily says: Oh sooooooooooooo cuuuuuuuuuuuuuuute!!!!

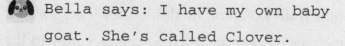 Bella says: Got to go and help with milking now.

Emily says: Yuck. Goats are cute but only on the top.

After I say goodbye to Bella I think about what she said. She's right, a real friend wouldn't care. But you have to get someone to be your *starter* friend before they become your real friend. A starter friend would take one look at our house and decide to start somewhere else. I go to inspect the living room – after all, Mum has tidied up a bit. Maybe it's not as bad as I think. Unfortunately it's worse. Dad has brought a load of copper pipes home from work and he thinks they'll get stolen if he leaves them in his shed so they are now in the living room too. You can sit on the sofa, as long as you can limbo dance quite well.

"Don't touch them!" Mum says as she comes into the room, as if I am the sort of person who goes around looking for pipes to damage.

The thing is, friends don't mind your house

being a little bit of a mess. After all, everyone's house has some messy bits – but when you live in a mansion with servants you probably expect to be able to at least get from the front door to the sofa without doing a gym circuit.

I must sigh in just the right way because Mum says, "Are you all right?"

"I was thinking about asking Chloe round for tea," I say. Before I can finish off saying that I was only thinking it, and totally not going to do it, Mum jumps in.

"I'm sorry, love, but there is no way I can cope with having another kid in this house right now."

Honestly. She only has two children and one of them is tiny and the other one is practically grown-up. What would she do if she had to cope with being a proper mother, like Gracie McKenzie's who mostly has children coming out of her ears? (Oh no! Another Gran-ism.)

I decide to give Mum the look of deep

disappointment I have been practising for just such an occasion.

My mum is not the sort of mum who is kind of generally nice all the time. She does it in bits and pieces when she's got time, which at the moment she hasn't much. But now she is obviously feeling a little bit like she has a spare couple of minutes because she says, "I tell you what, why don't I meet you from school tomorrow and we can take Chloe to Betty's Cafe for tea. She can get picked up from there a bit later."

Result! You get loads nicer food at Betty's Cafe than you do in my house and Chloe will think it is much better than just going round Zuzanna's for tea. It's practically going out for dinner, much more Chloe's sort of thing. To make sure Mum can't change her mind I give her a big hug and say, "Thank you," at least twice. Then I rush off to text Chloe.

CHAPTER TWENTY-ONE

Don't Mention the Carrot Cake

(Tea for) Tuesday

Chloe was in a very friendly mood at school today. I think I might just be in with a chance after all. Zuzanna must be really mad that I have got in with a last-minute "Come for tea," especially as it is a going to be a cafe type of tea.

At lunchtime Chloe and I were chatting when Zuzanna came over and said, "Did you have a nice time at my house last night?"

Chloe said, "Yes, it was OK, thanks. You have got a really small bedroom though, haven't you?"

Zuzanna just looked a bit unhappy and went off again. I almost felt sorry for her but not quite. After all, it is coming down to the nitty-gritty now (that is a Dad-ism, not a Gran-ism, but I'd better not get into all that again).

After school Mum meets us outside with Yoda in the Baby Eco-Jogger Deluxe. Yoda is crying. Chloe starts to look less happy.

"Is it coming too?" Chloe asks, pointing at the buggy.

Mum does a wrinkly mouth. "Yes of course it – I mean *she* – is coming."

"Oh well. I expect she'll stop making that noise when she gets to the restaurant," Chloe says. "Where's your car?"

"We are walking," Mum says. "Come along." And she marches off with the Baby Eco-Jogger Deluxe while I link arms with Chloe and jolly her along in the right direction. After a few minutes' walking while Chloe tells me all about the new plasma TV she's getting in her bedroom, we arrive outside Betty's Cafe.

"Is that it?" Chloe says in a way which sounds like someone has just given her half a fish finger when she was expecting cod and chips.

"It's our favourite place, isn't it, Emily?" Mum says.

"I ... err ... yes. Our favourite out of all the cafes between home and school. Obviously not our totally favourite cafe in the whole world."

Mum frowns at me but I pretend not to notice. We go in and sit at our favourite table near the window. Mum and I come here quite a lot. Mum always has a pot of tea and a slice of carrot cake and I always have a homemade lemonade and a slice of carrot cake. It's sort of traditional. Mrs Patterson, the lady who runs the cafe, comes hurrying over when we arrive as she is so pleased to see the baby.

"Oh! She's beautiful!" she says about thirty-seven times – which is not actually true, she is still quite weird looking, but there's not a lot else you can say about babies. I have noticed that people mostly say, "Isn't she beautiful?" "Look at her little fingers," and, "Is she good?" After that they start talking about the weather.

"The usual, is it?" says Mrs Patterson.

"I'll have a menu please," Chloe says. Mrs Patterson looks at her in surprise, as if she's just asked for something very complicated. She goes off and comes back with a tatty-looking menu and hands it to Chloe.

"I'll come back in a minute," she says, which is very lucky because Chloe opens the menu and says:

"Ew! They have cake made of carrots! That is gross – and one made of beetroot. This place is completely abnormal."

I am very glad Mrs Patterson doesn't

hear. She might have thrown us out. I have seen her get very cross with someone who wanted extra cream on their scone. Mum gives me a look which means, "We need to have a little chat later," and I try to do one back which says, "I don't know what you're on about."

Then Mum says, "The carrot cake is very nice, Chloe. Why don't you give it a try?"

"Do I look like a rabbit?" Chloe says.

Mum takes a deep breath but I leap in quickly with, "Perhaps we should have a cheese and ham toastie, Chloe," which fortunately seems to be the right thing to say to calm everyone down.

"So, girls," Mum says once we have ordered, "are you all ready for the Tudor Times Time-Travel Trip tomorrow?"

"Yes, Emily and I are going to be partners, aren't we?" Chloe says.

"R-really?" I splutter. "I mean absolutely. *Totally boatally.*"

I am so pleased I can hardly eat my toastie (and also it is very hot). Mum chatters away about the baby and Chloe is too busy eating to say much and for just a few minutes I think, *FINALLY EVERYTHING IS GOING RIGHT, there is no way Zuzanna can make a comeback now. Gross-Out is just a distant blob of annoyingness. Zuzanna will have to be his partner!* Then I get that funny little feeling where I feel a bit sorry for Zuzanna again but I take a big bite of my toastie and munch the thought away.

Mrs Patterson comes over to see if everything is all right.

"Fine thanks," I say through a mouthful of toastie and for once that might actually be true.

"I thought I recognised you!" Mrs Patterson is looking right at Chloe. "You are the one who came in and bought that big Victoria sponge yesterday morning, aren't you? Well I hope you enjoyed it!"

"It was OK, wasn't it, Emily?" Chloe says.

I choke a bit on my lemonade.

Mum smiles and says, "What Victoria sponge?" and looks as if she is trying to work something out. Fortunately at that moment the door of the cafe swings open and it is Chloe's servant. She is wearing a white overall with "Maid Service Ltd" sewn on it.

"Thank you so much for looking after Chloe," she says to Mum. "Sorry we must dash off, I'm borrowing my boss's car and he needs it back."

Mum frowns a little at the four-by-four outside the window, and I am thinking, *Please don't start on an eco-roll,* but it's OK because she just smiles and says, "It's been a pleasure."

And I think, *That really is a white lie.*

"Gotta go!" Chloe says. "See you tomorrow, partner!" and she smacks me on the shoulder and runs out to the car.

Thank goodness that's over. It was getting a bit dodgy towards the end, but finally I am in a Gross-Out-free zone. I am just sitting, smiling and staring at the door, when suddenly it bursts open and it is Chloe's servant again.

"Chloe left her bag!" she says, snatching it up from the floor next to my chair. "I swear that daughter of mine would forget her head if it wasn't stuck on. She's in her own fantasy world most of the time," and she dashes out again.

I stare after her as the door closes.

Daughter?!

CHAPTER TWENTY-TWO

Partners in Pillowcases

Wednesday – Tudor Times
Time-Travel Trip time

I am wearing a large, white (except for a small tea stain) pillowcase with cut-out holes for arms. Mum has cut down one of her old skirts to make a kirtle – it is very itchy, but Mum says Tudors were often itchy. I also have one of Gran's old aprons on which she says she got free with a box of teabags in

1962. Apparently it used to be pink but it is now a very realistic peasant grey. Gran has also made a "coif" cap out of a large hanky and I am very much hoping it has never been used. The cap is a bit big and keeps slipping over my eyes but all in all I do look quite Tudor. Probably, mostly like a poor, sad, itchy girl with only an old pillowcase and hanky to wear, but still quite Tudor. I also have a small stash of garibaldi biscuits as my mum refused to say I had a turnip allergy. Garibaldi biscuits were all I could find though and I think I might end up preferring pottage.

Last night I tried to talk to Bella but when I got online there was just a message:

🐶 Bella says: Hi, Emily. Really sorry, won't be online tonight. Clover has been poorly and I am looking after her. Speak soon. Bella.

Typical. Unforeseen circumstances just when I didn't see them coming. I thought, *I bet no one else in the world has to sit and worry all on their own all evening just because their best friend has to look after a sick goat.* Then I felt a bit mean because it was not very nice about Clover being poorly.

So I had a long think, all by myself. This is what I decided:

a) Chloe is a big liar.

b) Gross-Out Gavin might be stupid, disgusting and annoying but at least he is honest about it.

c) I would rather be partners with a stupid, disgusting annoying person than a liar (just).

So this morning I am going to tell Chloe that I don't want to be her partner any more. She can be partners with Zuzanna.

Actually, having to walk all the way to school dressed in a pillowcase, a grey apron and a hanky is so embarrassing that I don't have any spare brain particles left to use thinking about Chloe.

Especially as we have to be there by 8.15 a.m. which has "messed up the baby's routine". I didn't know she had a routine – she is the only person in our house who does.

Once I get to school, however, I start feeling very nervous. I am not at all looking forward to telling Chloe what I think of her, but I am going to do it. When I get in to class, though, Chloe is not there. Which is odd because we are a bit late, of course.

Mrs Lovetofts is dressed like a Tudor peasant lady. Zuzanna's mum has come as a "helper" which mostly means fussing about and laughing too loudly. She is wearing a red dress with a frilly ruff round the neck.

"Like Anne Boleyn," she says, doing a twirl. I think she looks more like Henry VIII to be honest.

Then I see Zuzanna. She is wearing a cut-up pillowcase a bit like mine. I decide to be brave and tell her she can have Chloe as her partner and I am about to go over to her when suddenly she is over to me.

"Emily," she says, "I have just come to say that you can be Chloe's trip partner."

At least she realises she's been beaten. "I know," I say, "but it's OK. I don't want to be. You can."

"No. No worries. You go with Chloe. I'll go with Gross-Out Gavin."

"No, that's fine." I say, surprised. "I don't mind at all."

"Neither do I. You can go with Chloe."

"No. I'll go with Gross-Out."

"No," she says, "I said it first!"

"Look," I say. "I'm trying to be nice here!"

She throws her hands up in the air. "Well that makes a change!"

"Sit down please, Year Six," Mrs Lovetofts says firmly.

I stomp over to my table. Really, that girl is just

a total pain. And then I notice a very surprising thing.

Alfie Balfour.

Alfie Balfour is not supposed to be here. Perhaps he is going to visit his nan later. But he is – and he's wearing a Tudor costume so he must be actually going on the Tudor Times Time-Travel Trip. Which means . . .

"Now then," says Mrs Lovetofts, "there are a few things we need to sort out. Alfie's nan has been let out of her special old people's home early, so Alfie is able to come on the school trip after all. So that means Alfie and Gavin will be partners and Emily – you can go with Zuzanna."

"No, Miss!" Zuzanna and I say together.

"That's settled, girls," says Mrs Lovetofts firmly *again*. Perhaps she's been taking lessons from Mr Meakin.

Zuzanna stops glaring at me long enough to ask, "But, Miss – where's Chloe?"

"Chloe won't be joining us till later," Mrs Lovetofts says. "Her mother phoned to say she'd be late. She's going to catch up with us at Ickwell Hall."

We all go to line up for the bus and I have to stand next to Zuzanna. Mr Meakin walks up and down the row. He is wearing some very silly short trousers and long socks and a floppy hat.

"Prithee behave yourselves, you horrible little beggars," he shouts.

Zuzanna's mum giggles but no one else does because he is just being himself really. Daniel Waller is already crying because he thought the coach would be a Tudor one pulled by horses, when it is actually just a Brewster's Bus. I have to sit next to Zuzanna but I just stare out of the window and ignore her. It is a bit annoying, though, because I really do want to ask her why she has changed her mind about being Chloe's partner, but it is not that easy to start up a conversation with your sworn enemy, even when they are your bus partner. Mr Meakin gets on and stands at the front and does a big talk about "representing the school" and "behaving in a dignified manner" and I think maybe he should look in the mirror.

And then we are off.

Mrs Lovetofts tries to get us all singing some of the ancient songs she has been teaching us but mostly she ends up singing by herself and then Alfie Balfour sings some rude words to "I'm Henery the Eighth, I Am", and Mr Meakin says singing is banned for the rest of the day.

Then Gracie McKenzie is sick so we have to stop the bus so she can have some fresh air, although it is the people left on the bus who really need fresh air. Fortunately, with all this going on I don't have to spend a lot of time ignoring Zuzanna as properly ignoring someone is very hard work.

Amy-Lee gets bored waiting for Gracie to go the right colour again and wanders up the bus with Yeah-Yeah Yasmin tagging along behind.

"Got any chocolate?" Amy-Lee says when she gets to our seat.

"Yeah. Chocolate. Yeah," Yeah-Yeah Yasmin says.

"No," I say, "just garibaldi biscuits."

"Gary Barlow biscuits?" Amy-Lee says. "Cool! Give us some then."

"What about you?" she says to Zuzanna, grabbing her bag. "Got anything?"

Before Zuzanna can answer I grab Zuzanna's bag back and say, "Gary Barlow biscuits are from both of us – if you want them leave us alone, otherwise you get nothing."

I am very worried that my mouth has just done a very brave thing before my brain could stop it.

Then out of nowhere Mr Meakin appears and says, "Is everything all right here, girls? Where did you get those biscuits, Amy-Lee? I hope you haven't been demanding foodstuffs with menaces!"

I'm not quite sure what

he is on about but I think Amy-Lee is probably on her last chance with Mr Meakin so I say, "It's OK, Sir. I gave them to her."

"That's all right then," he says, fixing Amy-Lee with a stern stare before walking back down the bus.

"Now go away," I say to Amy-Lee.

"All right, keep your wig on," she says.

"Yeah. Wig on. Yeah," Yeah-Yeah Yasmin says.

And they go off to pick on someone else.

Zuzanna looks at me with big eyes. "Wow. Thanks."

"That's OK," I say, like standing up to bullies is something I do all the time, and I shove my hands under my bag so she can't see them shaking.

Zuzanna is quiet for a minute, then she says, "So ... why didn't you want to be partners with Chloe?"

"Why didn't you?" I ask.

But before we can get any further the bus turns into the drive of Ickwell Hall.

CHAPTER TWENTY-THREE

Pottering About

Wednesday - Ickwell Hall

The coach bumps down a long driveway and everyone near the front of the bus suddenly starts shouting "Ooh!" and "Look!"

I stand up to see what it is we are supposed to be ooohing and looking at and I just have time to see the flags of Ickwell Hall sticking up above the trees before the coach swings into the car park and

I end up sitting down again. Unfortunately I don't sit down in my seat but on Zuzanna.

"Mosh ish!" she says through a mouthful of my kirtle.

"What?" I say.

Zuzanna elbows me off her lap. "I said, 'Watch it!'"

Luckily we don't have time to get into another argument because Mr Meakin is standing up at the front of the coach.

"Prithee, everyone! Stop-eth messing about and hark," he shouts.

I don't think many people really understand him but it doesn't matter because once Mr Meakin starts talking everyone shuts up anyway. "Thank you," he says and tries really hard to do a smiley face, which always makes him look a bit creepy but is somehow even worse coming from under a Tudor hat.

"Today is going to be very educational. We will

be meeting lots of Tudor folk and will of course get to try the famous pottage! Now, I will go to meet-eth with the Head of Tudor Experiences and will-eth leave you in the capable hands of Mistress Lovetofts ... eth," he says with a little laugh at his own Tudor-ishness before ducking out of the coach. He must worry that he's been a bit too jolly though because he suddenly pops up again and says, "And remember, I expect impeccable behaviour, at all times, or you will have me to answer to later."

Mrs Lovetofts give us all a big smile and does a head count to make sure no one has run away yet.

There is a bit of a panic when it turns out someone is missing but everything is OK when Gracie pops up from under her seat clutching the drinks bottle she had dropped. Mrs Lovetofts does one more count just to be on the safe side, and thank goodness no one decides to do up their shoelaces, so finally we are allowed off the coach.

Outside in the car park Mrs Lovetofts asks if anyone needs the toilet. Everyone puts their hand up, mostly because no one wants to wait until we are in the Tudor village in case they have to go in a bucket and empty it in the street. There is a lot more queuing up and head counting until finally we get to go inside the gates.

Ickwell Hall is not white with black beams; it is very big and made of red brick, with large windows and little towers with flags on. In fact it is nothing at all like a Tudor building, and I am beginning to wonder if we have come to the wrong place and any minute now some rich lord or banker is going to come running out shouting, "Get those peasants off my front lawn." Mrs Lovetofts helpfully explains that rich Tudors lived in buildings that didn't look like any of the ones we've been finding out about and I am glad Chloe is not here to say, "Told you that homework was a waste of time."

"Ickwell Hall is a fabulous example of sixteenth-century architecture," says Mrs Lovetofts. "Wonderfully preserved, an authentic Tudor gem! However, it is closed today while they have new broadband cables installed. So instead we will be walking in the grounds and enjoying the fabulous Tudor village life reconstructions."

Then she explains that we will be split into groups with an adult leader. "You will do a morning of exciting living-history activities with your group, then we will meet for lunch and an afternoon of archery!

"Alfie and Gavin, you will be with Mr Meakin." Alfie groans but it is their own fault because they always mess about.

"Emily Sparkes, you will also be with Mr Meakin." Now it is my turn to groan. It is very unfair because I never mess about, but I get put with people who do mess about to set a good example – that is the strange way teachers' minds work. Zuzanna, Babette and Joshua also get put in Team Meakin and we get Zuzanna's mum as a helper. She gives me a bit of a stern glance as she walks across, and I know she still blames me for the cake catastrophe. Then it is time to meet the Tudors.

Mr Meakin holds up his clipboard and says, "Right. Fall in, men," and as usual no one really knows what he means but it doesn't matter as he is off down the path and calling for us to follow him to "the pottery".

The pottery, or "Potterie" as it says on the sign because Tudor people were rubbish at spelling, turns out to be mostly a load of old sheds around a big brick igloo, which is apparently the kiln where the pots are baked. There are several people wandering about, dressed as Tudors only in proper clothes, not pillowcases. I go over to see a woman who is pushing clay around a table. She seems to have bright orange hands. I am just wondering if she's going to make something other than a mess when she speaks.

"Good morrow, young maid!" she says.

Oh no! I really don't want to speak to her.

"Mayhap thou has noticed my hands. The clay stains fair skin, but such is the life of a potter." She smiles. I know she is just being friendly but it is very difficult to have a conversation with someone who is basically a museum exhibit. Anyway I don't know how to say "don't worry, orange hands are cool with me" in Tudor. I look around for someone to help me but everyone else is watching a man putting pots in the igloo.

"Prithee tell, hast thee walked far this day?" she says and now I'm going to have to say something or I'll seem really rude.

I can feel myself going red and I manage to splutter, "I've only walked from the coach."

"Ah, thou hast a coach. Truly thou must be a fine lady!"

"No! No, it's not that sort of coach," I say but then I feel a bit confused. I mean she's only dressed up, right? She's not really Tudor. She must know. And now I am starting to worry that maybe she's a bit, you know . . . strange. I mean, what sort of person does this anyway? Gets all dressed up as a Tudor in the morning to go to work – imagine if that was my mum going off in the morning saying, "Prithee enjoy school and mayhap we'll have pizza tonight." Not that that's likely to happen – my mum finds it hard enough to get up and dressed as an ordinary person most days.

I have had enough of the clay lady; also I am not sure if I should be talking to strange Tudors on my own, so I quickly walk off to see what other embarrassing situations I can get into, and I manage to find one almost immediately.

"Good morrow!" calls a very jolly man in a big blouse.

Oh no, not again. I wish all these Tudors would stop being so friendly.

"Err. Good morrow," I reply, which seems to be the right thing to say, or maybe the wrong thing as he gives me a big smile and says:

"I prithee sit down and try your skill on the potter's wheel." He gives me a jolly slap on the back and shoves me in the direction of a muddy stool in front of a wheel with a lump of clay in the middle.

"No, it's OK, really," I try to protest.

"Thou speaketh in a strange tongue," he says, and I am thinking, *He should mayhap listen to himself.*

"Oh yes, very good idea. Let's see what you can do, Emily," says Mr Meakin in a head-teacher-type voice, which doesn't sound right coming from a man in baggy pantaloons.

"Everyone, Emily is going to make a pot!"

Zuzanna's mum calls and the others hurry over, glad of something more exciting to do than watching clay dry.

"No, I really don't want—" but the Tudor man smiles his jolly smile and says something about not understandering-eth me or whatever. He presses a pedal and the wheel starts spinning round. I have to make a grab for the clay which is threatening to go shooting off the wheel.

"That's right, maid. Use your hands to draw the pot," he urges and although I have no clue what to do I can't let go or the clay will go flying. I try to shape the spinning lump into a pot shape but it just goes all floppy and wobbly. The others start laughing.

"That's not a pot, it's a pancake," shouts Alfie.

"Thou needs to control the clay, maid," says the Tudor man, like it's something I haven't thought of.

"I'm trying!" I say.

"Let me have a go!" says Alfie, pushing in next to me.

"But I can't let go," I protest as he tries to nudge me out of the way.

"I bet I can do it," he says, making a grab for the clay and knocking me off balance. My stool wobbles and I let go of the clay which goes flying off the wheel, through the air and slaps right across Zuzanna's face.

"*Mwaaawhgh!*" says Zuzanna.

"Flipping heck!" says the Tudor man. "I mean, gadzooks!"

There is a lot of fuss separating out Zuzanna from the clay. The Tudor lady gives her an old rag to wipe her face with, although it just sort of smears it around. Her mum tells her clay is very good for the skin but Zuzanna looks as if she wants to put someone in the stocks and throw mouldy veg at them, and I think that person is me.

I have a very strange feeling though, one that I have never had before. I am feeling sorry for Zuzanna. A few days ago I would have been quite pleased to see her get slapped in the face with a lump of wet clay, but now I don't feel quite the same.

The Tudor man gives me a bowl of water to wash my hands, which have turned bright orange. "It will fade in a day or so," he says, handing me a rag.

Zuzanna walks past me with her mum who is going to take her to the Ye Olde First Aid Tente to make sure she isn't suffering from any further pottery complications. Her mum gives me a very frosty look.

"Sorry, Zuzanna," I say, but I don't think she hears me, as she is getting clay out of her ear.

"I think," Mr Meakin says, "this would be a good time to move on to the next activity."

CHAPTER TWENTY-FOUR

Potion Problems

Wednesday - Ickwell Hall - still

"The apothecary was like a doctor," Mr Meakin explains as we go into an old barn, "or a pharmacist – basically they made potions and things to try to make people better. But if you have a headache, best not mention it – they rubbed people's heads with a hangman's noose to get rid of that." He laughs his creepy laugh and I think head teachers have a very different sense of humour to ordinary people. I am also wondering if the apothecary has anything to cure bright orange hands.

Inside the barn it is a little gloomy but actually smells really nice. Big bunches of dried flowers and herbs are hanging from the ceiling and an old woman is grinding things up in a stone bowl.

"Wonder what she's got in there?" whispers Joshua.

"She's an old witch," grins Gross-Out. "Toads' eyes and bat wings."

"It is the flower of the elder and the calendula, young man, and there is no sorcery involved," says the old woman who has obviously taken a potion to give her superhuman hearing. Gavin looks at his feet and the rest of us gather round to see what she is making.

"Suffer ye from the lice of the hair?" she says to Alfie who is scratching the back of his head. "I have some tobacco juice for that."

Alfie says, "No, that was last week. It's just this stupid hat is too itchy." But I notice Mr Meakin takes a small step away from him.

Then she shows us some snake skins and dead mice she uses for treating whooping cough, and I get that funny feeling again where I think, *Does she really do this or is she still pretending?* I decide I will not cough till we get out, just in case.

Then she gets on to a nicer bit. She shows us the different herbs and flowers that she uses and lets us have a turn crushing them in the pestle and mortar and adding oil to make our own sweet-smelling potions, and even though I am worrying a bit about Zuzanna, I am actually having a really nice time. I think maybe I could make some potions at home – especially if it made our house smell a bit better and not mostly of nappies.

In fact, I think it's a pity Zuzanna is missing this bit because she would probably like it too. I might make a bit extra for her.

Everything is going fine-ish until Gross-Out and Alfie start to get bored (because they are making things which smell nice and so probably don't have any use for them) and begin wandering about the room. After a few minutes, Gross-Out sidles up to me and says, "What are you making, Emily?" but I am not being fooled by that. Gross-Out never takes an interest in what you are doing except when he's about to mess it up. I spin round just in time to notice that he is about to drop something down my back.

I try to duck out of the way but accidentally knock into him and he stumbles sideways. The thing he was about to drop on me flies out of his hand and sails gracefully through the air before plopping into Babette's mixing bowl.

I really didn't realise she could scream that loud – she should do sound effects for scary films.

"Get it out! Get it out!" she yells, dancing about and waving her arms in the air.

There is a lot of shouting and laughing and Mr Meakin jumps up from where he has been dozing in a chair in the corner and tries to work out what's going on.

I peer cautiously into Babette's bowl and see a very tiny and completely dead mouse. It's quite cute really – it has a sort of surprised look on its face, like it didn't mean to be dead but just got that way by accident. Babette clearly doesn't think it's at all cute, though, as she is still screaming even though the apothecary lady tells her to "be calm" and keeps waving a bunch of herbs over her head.

Just at that moment, Zuzanna and her mum come back.

"Oh dear, whatever has happened now?" Zuzanna's mum says, eyeing me suspiciously.

"It be the hysterics," says the apothecary, "and camomile will not becalm her."

So Zuzanna's mum swaps Zuzanna for Babette and takes her off to the Ye Olde First Aid Tente to have a glass of water and get over her "mental excitement".

The apothecary lady is not happy. Apparently putting dead mouse in with ground elderflower and marigold is a sure-fire way of messing up its healing qualities and it will all have to be binned. Those of us who have potions without mouse in are allowed to put them in a little bottle to take home. I have done a spare one for Zuzanna but I don't think now is a very good time to give it to her. I hope she hasn't looked in a mirror because her face is as orange as my hands.

"Thank you, it's been very interesting," says Mr Meakin to the apothecary lady, who has gone to sit down and rub her head with a hangman's noose. "I think," he continues, "this would be a good time to move on to the next activity."

The final activity of the morning is meeting the pottage makers. We all walk along a path to a clearing in the woods where there is a campfire with a big cauldron on it – I get a bit worried as it looks a lot like a picture book of Hansel and Gretel I used to have when I was little, and I wonder if we should have left a trail of breadcrumbs or something. Fortunately all the women standing around the tables appear to be just chopping vegetables and no one is wearing a tall black hat.

"Come hither, child," says a very thin, bony lady standing next to me, "and help me chop vegetables for the pot." Mr Meakin gives me a bit of a shove forward and I have to go to help even though I really don't want to because I did not come on a school trip just to do something I can be easily forced into doing at home. And just my luck it is the onion-chopping lady. I spend the next ten minutes crying worse than Daniel Waller when he's forgotten his packed lunch, while everyone else gets to do something much more fun like washing turnips and peeling carrots. Then everything gets slurped into the pot.

"Carrots, turnips, onions, beans and garlic," says the bony lady. "An excellent pottage shall we eat this day," and I am thinking that it all sounds very healthy but the bony lady might want to follow hers up with a goode olde sticky toffee pudding or else she might disappear altogether.

Once the pottage is bubbling away we all get a chance to stir it. I am very careful with my stirring as I have already been in two disasters today and Gran says they always come in threes. Mind you, she says that about buses as well ... and colds ... and people having babies – in fact come to think of it she says it about most things.

Still, I am very glad when it is time to go to meet up with the others for lunch and to finally get a bit of a break from slaving over a hot cauldron.

We have to line up to wash our hands in a bowl of water. I do not think this is very hygienic because everyone is using the same water and I have to go last in case I make the water orange. Unfortunately, the orange stays on my hands, which makes me worry even more about Zuzanna's orange face and whether she's looked in the mirror yet.

Mrs Lovetofts is flapping about trying very hard to get people excited about the "living history lunch", but it is not easy to get enthusiastic about overcooked vegetable mush.

A Tudor person hands me a wooden bowl and I hold it out to get a big dollop of pottage. It looks a bit grey and smells of turnips (no, I didn't know what they smelled like either, but trust me, they smell like the word sounds). Another Tudor person hands me a wooden spoon and I wander off to look for somewhere to sit. I don't really want to sit with the others. Bella would tell me off for being "unsociable", but sometimes, when you have orange hands, no best friend and a big bowl of pottage to eat, it's easier to be on your own.

I take my bowl and go to sit on a tree stump that someone has helpfully left lying about. The pottage is very thick and gooey but actually quite nice – turnips taste a lot better than they smell.

"Do you mind if I sit here too?" says a voice next to me. I look up and I am totally surprised to see that the voice belongs to Zuzanna.

"Mov corsh," I splutter through a mouthful of pottage, "jats showkay."

She does very well at understanding though and sits down. We don't say anything for a minute, partly because I am so used to not talking to her that I don't know where to begin, but mostly because my mouth is stuck up with pottage.

"I didn't want to sit over there," she says. "Gross-Out keeps laughing at my orange face."

When I can finally get some words out I say, "I'm really sorry."

"Don't worry, it wasn't your fault, it was stupid Alfie Balfour," she says, which is true but I didn't think she realised. "My mum's not happy though, she says this trip is a health and safety disaster. Apparently Small Emily B. got flicked in the eye by a morris dancer's handkerchief and will have to wear an eyepatch for a week. There's a ten-minute queue outside the Ye Olde First Aid Tente."

And I think, *This is the longest conversation I have ever had with Zuzanna without an argument starting.*

"I made you a flower and herb potion," I say, handing her the bottle, "so you didn't miss out too much."

"Thanks," she smiles. "At least I missed out on Babette screaming."

"Camomile would not becalm her," I laugh, and she laughs too – which feels very strange, but nice.

We finish our pottage and then she slips a couple of chocolate biscuits out from under her apron. "I sneaked these in, in case the pottage was too terrible – thanks for saving them from Amy-Lee this morning. It's a pity you had to give up your Gary Barlow biscuits. Are they really nice?"

"Well, they are my gran's favourites," I say, because I don't want her to think I haven't made any sacrifices.

"I wonder where Chloe is," Zuzanna says. It's strange, I realise I have hardly thought about Chloe all morning. She doesn't seem that important any more.

"She seemed all right yesterday," I say and then I don't say any more in case Zuzanna is cross about us taking Chloe out for tea.

"Oh yes. You took her to Betty's Cafe, didn't you?"

"It wasn't much fun," I say quickly.

"I bet it wasn't," she says.

I have to ask her – I am completely dying to know.

"So ..." I say, "why didn't you want to be her partner any more?"

Zuzanna wrinkles up her orange face. "Because she totally tells lies all the time. It was bad enough about the Victoria sponge, but then my mum talked to her mum when she came to pick her up from my house and found out everything. Her mum is a cleaner and works for an American man who has a big white car and a big house, but they don't live there, and I bet she never went to Magnolia Hall. I bet the place doesn't even exist!"

"I know," I say, "and all the time she was pretending her mum was *her* servant."

"So she never had cookery lessons with Jamie Oliver," Zuzanna adds.

"And she doesn't have a pony either."

"Or two swimming pools."

We are both quiet for a bit. It's quite a lot to take in. I stare across the field and watch Mr Meakin telling Amy-Lee Langer off for throwing pottage at the peacocks.

"But why did she tell all those lies?" I say at last.

"I don't know. Maybe she thought we wouldn't like her if she was ordinary like us."

At that moment, there is a loud shriek. I look up to see Chloe Clarke running across the field towards us, waving her arms.

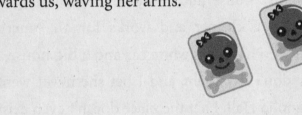

CHAPTER TWENTY-FIVE

The Greatest Archer on the Estate

Wednesday. Still here

"What is she wearing?" Zuzanna says. "She looks like a . . . a raspberry pavlova!"

I am not entirely sure what a raspberry pavlova is. We don't get many desserts in our house. But she definitely looks like some sort of pudding. She is wearing a long, deep-pink dress with cream and white frills all over it and big puffy satin sleeves.

"I suppose it is some sort of genuine vintage gown that her mother got from an exclusive shop," I say.

"Emily – her mother is a cleaner!" snaps Zuzanna.

"Oh yes, I keep forgetting," I say, feeling a bit confused again.

Chloe reaches us and says breathlessly, "Hi, girls! Sorry I'm so late. Wow, what is this *freaky* place?" She looks around. "Like, it's so totally old-fashioned! There are like people living in huts and I passed some guys back there saying like 'good morrow' and stuff. Like, what century are they from?!"

"The sixteenth century, Chloe. It's Tudor, remember?" I say. "Why aren't you wearing an apron and hat?"

She gives us a big grin. "You are never going to believe what happened."

"No, probably not," Zuzanna says, rolling her eyes.

Chloe glances in her direction. "Nice tan," she says. "Lend me that a minute." She grabs the shawl from Zuzanna's shoulders and puts it on a log before sitting down. "I am so not allowed to get my dress muddy."

"But why are you wearing that dress?" I say. "It's not even a bit Tudor."

"OK – ready for the big news? My mum got married – to her boss! I was really hoping it would happen for ages and then they said we were going to have a little celebration – but it turned out to be a wedding! I've just come from the registry office. I was a fabulous bridesmaid, everyone said so!" she says, jumping up and twirling her dress around.

Chloe beams her big, shiny white smile in my direction but I don't feel even a little bit pleased that she likes me any more. I am so fed up with her lies.

"If you're supposed to be a bridesmaid, what are you doing here?" I say.

"Mum agreed to drop me off so she can do some last-minute packing – tonight we fly to Goa – for the honeymoon!"

"I don't believe it," I say.

"And neither do I!" Zuzanna says.

"I know. I couldn't believe it either. It's so cool, isn't it?"

"No, I mean I *really* don't believe you, Chloe," I say, getting exasperated. "Your mum didn't get married to anyone. Your mum is a cleaner! We know."

"Not any more – now she's Mrs Van Hilton!"

"Chloe, this is just another one of your stories," snaps Zuzanna. "Why don't you just tell the truth? Like your mum bought the wrong sort of costume and you're late because the car wouldn't start or something."

"Stories?" Chloe says, looking genuinely surprised. "I don't make things up."

"You said your mum was your servant!" I say.

"Did I? You probably got the wrong end of the

stick. Anyway, it doesn't matter because now she's Mrs Van Hilton we'll have to get some new servants."

Zuzanna sighs. "But you said you had swimming pools and horses."

"We do!" she says. "Mr Van Hilton – sorry, I mean, my new *stepdaddy* – is very rich."

"Oh, this is hopeless!" says Zuzanna.

"*Totally*," I say, and Zuzanna gives me a sharp look. "I mean, *completely*."

Chloe smiles and says, "Oh, girls. Don't let's argue. I insisted that Mum dropped me off to say goodbye to my friends."

"Goodbye?" I say, confused.

"Yes. I won't be coming back. I'm sorry. I know you'll miss me."

"Don't tell me," I say, "you're going to Mag Hall."

"Totally!" Chloe says. "But hey, don't be sad – you've got each other now. You two are very similar, you know."

Zuzanna and I look at each other. "Really?" we both say together.

"Yes," Chloe says. "Sensible, not very imaginative and . . . slightly orange. But totally nice underneath it all."

Then suddenly she leaps up and gives us both a big hug and I get a face full of scratchy raspberry-pavlova lace.

"It's been fun, hasn't it?" she says and I am still trying to work out which part she's talking about when Mr Meakin announces it's time for the archery event.

"I'd better come with you for a bit, just till my mum get here," Chloe says.

"But you're not even in Tudor costume," I say.

"Oh, don't fuss, Emily. I'll just pretend to be the lady of the manor," she says. "It suits me better than being a peasant like you two."

"I am Jack Smith," says a man with a feather in his hat, which is disappointing because I was sure he was going to say, "I am Robin Hood."

He picks up a huge bow which is almost as big as he is. He turns and looks at us all. "I am a Master Archer. The greatest archer on the estate." Which sounds a bit showy-offy to me and I think he'll get on well with Chloe.

"Is that not so, brothers?" he says to the small group of other archers who are standing around him like the Merry Men.

"Aye. 'Tis well, Jack," they say.

Jack Smith pulls an arrow from a sack (which is apparently called a "quiver", probably because that's what people do when he points his bow and arrow at them), puts it in his bow and aims it towards the target at the other end of the field, then he draws back his bow and lets go. The arrow flies through the air with a swishing, whizzing

 sound and lands right in the bullseye of the target. He turns round to us and says, "See?" with a smug grin.

Lots of people say, "Oooh," and, "Wow!" and he even gets a round of applause, but really I think, *It's just his job.* I mean, he's bound to be good at it if he does it every day. My dad is good at stopping toilets leaking but he doesn't expect a round of applause every time. Still, lots of people, mostly Mr Meakin, are very excited about having a go.

"I'll kick off proceedings, shall I?" says Mr Meakin, grabbing a bow from the nearest archer. And I am just thinking I don't know much about archery but I'm sure you don't have a kick-off, when Mr Meakin's arrow goes flying past me into a tree and I start thinking this might be a good time to ask to go to the toilet.

"I think ye shouldst stick to the schoolroom,

Sir," says Jack Smith and all the Merry Men laugh. Mr Meakin hastily hands back his bow with a little noise that's a bit like a laugh but also sounds like he forgot how to do it properly.

"So," says Jack Smith, "who wants to be the next to try to take my crown? Let's see what the boys can do, shall we?"

Joshua is first – he manages to shoot the arrow but only about a metre into the grass.

Jack Smith snorts. "Methinks I will keep my name as the greatest archer on the estate today. What think ye, men?"

"Aye, 'tis well," repeat the Merry Men.

Gross-Out Gavin is disqualified before he gets a go for trying to pick Alfie's nose with an arrow, then Alfie's arrow shoots out backwards and hits Daniel Waller in the knee which makes him cry and he has to go to off the Ye Olde First Aid Tente with Zuzanna's mum.

I am just thinking about my dad turning up at

someone's house in a feathery hat and announcing, "I am a Master Plumber. The greatest plumber on this housing estate," when suddenly it is my turn.

"A damsel! And with orange fingers. Methinks my reputation is safe!" says Jack Smith, handing me a bow. "What say you, men?"

"Aye. 'Tis well, Jack," say the Merry Men, but not as merrily as before.

Somehow you are supposed to hold the bow, hold the arrow, pull the string back and let the whole lot go just at the right moment. Really, you need to be an octopus. After a few tries I finally manage to get everything balanced, pull back hard on the string and suddenly let go. The bow twangs and the arrow drops on the grass by my feet.

"Ha!" laughs Jack Smith. "Maidens do not have the way with the bow. Jack Smith will never be bested by a maiden. What say ye, men?"

"Aye," says one.

"'Tis well," mutters another.

And I think, *It is a good job I do not have a way with the bow or Jack Smith might not survive very long.* Nicole, Babette and Gracie also all do very well making a nice twanging sound with the bow and dropping the arrow in the grass.

Then it is Zuzanna's turn. She doesn't do much to improve the image of maidens either – her arrow ends up behind her. Jack Smith giggles and says, "Go back to the wash house, that is maid's work! And methinks whilst there, ye should also wash thy face." And he roars with laughter.

Mrs Lovetofts gets a bit annoyed at that and says, "Now then, Mr Smith, all the children are trying their best."

This makes Jack laugh even more and he says, "Hark, men, the mistress hath scolded us!"

Mrs Lovetofts goes very red.

"I'm sure it's just genuine sixteenth-century humour," Mr Meakin says to her, looking like he wants to get back to the twenty-first century as soon as possible.

Amy-Lee and Yeah-Yeah are not allowed to do any more activities after the peacock and pottage incident so there is only Chloe left.

"The last of the day," says Jack Smith. "Truly methinks this is the worst band of archers we have ever had here, and Jack Smith remains the greatest archer on the estate – is that not so, brothers?"

"Aye, 'tis well," mutter one or two of the Merry Men, who are definitely sounding a bit fed up of hearing it.

"Oooh, 'tis a fine lady," grins Jack Smith as Chloe picks up the bow.

"Not only that, but I am an excellent archer – Magnolia Hall school champion three years running," says Chloe. "Personally taught by Jessica Ennis."

"But she does heptathlon," says Zuzanna.

"She branched out," says Chloe, selecting an arrow with care. "Stand clear."

"Go on, Chloe!" yells someone from the back.

"Yes, go on, you can do it!" calls another voice and then everyone is chanting:

"Chloe, Chloe."

Chloe puts the arrow in the bow – she really does look as if she knows what she's doing. A hush falls over the onlookers. Even Jack Smith looks a bit worried. Chloe pulls back the string and takes aim towards the target. She bites her lip in concentration and everyone holds their breath . . .

"Yoo-hoo! Chloe, love. Time to go!"

Everyone spins round to see Chloe's mother waving from across the field.

"Come on, love, we've got a plane to catch!"

Chloe shoves the bow and arrow at me. "Sorry, Emily, you'll have to take my turn. Totally gotta go – there's a bride over there in need of a maid!"

"Coming!" she yells and runs off towards her mum.

I watch in disbelief as Chloe's puffy pink dress

bobs off across the field. So she was telling the truth. I look across at Zuzanna but before I can give her a look which means "I totally don't get it!" Jack Smith is speaking again.

"So Mistress Orange-Hands taketh the challenge once more!"

I look down at the bow in my hands.

"She might surprise you," says Mrs Lovetofts.

"Yeah, go on, Emily, show him!" says a voice I am very surprised to realise is coming from Gross-Out Gavin. Suddenly everyone is shouting, "Go on, Emily!" and, "You can do it, Emily!"

"Verily I quaketh with fear!" laughs Jack Smith.

I am verily – I mean *totally* – quaking too. How come I get lumped with defending the reputation of the whole school? I can't shoot a bow – I'm not even sure I've got it the right way up.

"I, err, don't think—"

"Come on, Emily," calls Zuzanna, "do it for the orange people."

What choice do I have? I step forward in front of the target and put the arrow in the bow. Once again everyone goes very quiet. I take a deep breath and pull back the string, and then let the arrow fly.

CHAPTER TWENTY-SIX

An Invitation

Back home - to "normal" life

Apparently Jack Smith was still trying to get his hat down from the tree when we got back on the coach. If that peacock hadn't screeched just as I fired the arrow it might not have turned into disaster number three. And it was Jack's fault really – I mean, everyone was supposed to stay behind the safety line. I suppose he thought I couldn't manage

to shoot the arrow anyway so it would
be OK to nip across the front to collect his
olde lunch box. I am very glad it was not a worse
disaster – seriously injuring archery instructors is
not something I want to be famous for. Still, the
merry men thought it was brilliant – I think they
were getting completely fed up with Jack Smith
showing off as well.

"I never beheld such a shot as that," said one of
them. "Took the hat right off his head."

"Did you see his face? Such skill, Mistress," said
another one as he laughed and slapped me on
the back. "Mayhap we shouldst all dye our hands
orange!"

I think even Mr Meakin was secretly pleased,
although he did apologise on behalf of the school.
In fact everyone was very pleased with me – well,
except Jack Smith.

Zuzanna is not on the bus back from Ickwell
Hall. Her mum took her home in a taxi after going

to make a formal complaint to the Head of Tudor Experiences. She said she had "serious health and safety concerns about the whole day". Although I would have thought that meant it was very realistic – they didn't have much health or safety at all in Tudor times.

Funny – this morning I didn't want to sit next to Zuzanna but now I am thinking I would kind of like her to be here, which is a strange thing to think about your "sworn enemy". Mrs Lovetofts hands out souvenir Ickwell Hall rubbers and rulers and Alfie and Gavin do impressions of Jack Smith by whacking each other's hats off all the way home.

The coach drops us back at school and we all have to go inside, just to have the register taken and to make sure that no one has been left behind. I really think it would be a lot quicker if they just gave out all the children to the waiting parents and then worried if there was a spare parent left over at the end, but teachers never think like that.

We get home and I am completely worn out. I'm glad we don't go on school trips very often or I would be old before my time. I take off my Tudor stuff and put on my normal clothes and I definitely feel a lot better. I think I might be allergic to the sixteenth century.

But now a totally weird thing happens. I am just looking through my school bag to find the ruler and rubber to show Mum, when I find, right at the top of my bag, an envelope. An envelope that I have never seen before (Gran would like this – it's a bit Agatha Christie, isn't it?). I open it and inside there is a card:

Dear Emily,
    Please come to my roller skating party on Sept 4th.
    From 4–6 p.m. RSVP.
    From
    Zuzanna

I am very confused. Why is Zuzanna inviting me to her party? It's not till next year.

I am staring at the card and trying to work something out . . . and now it is completely dawning on me in a very uncomfortable sort of way. It is not an invitation for next year – it is an *old* invitation for this year! For her party at Rollerworld.

But I wasn't invited, was I?

But it says "Emily S." on the envelope . . .

I have a mini panic and drop the invitation on the floor. Zuzanna *did* invite me! Why didn't I find this invitation earlier? *Oh no!* And I totally didn't invite her to my party! But I *heard* her say she wasn't inviting me. And there wasn't an invitation in my tray. *I know.*

Thank goodness it's six o'clock. I so badly need to talk to Bella.

 Emily says: Bella, r u there?
I need help!!!!

Emily says: Bella — can you hear me?????

 Emily says: Well, obviously you can't hear me, unless you have developed some sort of super-hearing from living up a Welsh mountain and drinking goat's milk — but are you there?!!!!

 Bella says: Hi, Emily. What are you going on about?

 Emily says: Bella — it's unbelievable!!!!!!!!

 Bella says: How was the trip?

 Emily says: Oh, fine. Well, apart from the orange hands, the dead mouse potion and the archery accident — but GUESS WHAT?

Bella says: ???????????????

 Emily says: I found my party invitation from Zuzanna!

 Bella says: It's a bit late now.

 Emily says: I know, but where has it been? It just turned up in my school bag!

 Bella says: It was probably in there all along.

 Emily says: No, it can't have been, this is the new bag I got for my birthday.

 Bella says: So she did invite you after all.

 Emily says: But I don't understand. She said I was a "total pain". I heard her.

Bella says: What exactly did
you hear, Emily?

I am getting in a bit of a major mini panic now.
I try to think back. Zuzanna put an invitation to
her party in everyone's tray, but when I went to
get mine I didn't have one. Everyone was showing
each other so I just went to the toilet to get away. I
was in a cubicle when I heard Zuzanna and Babette
come in talking.

 Emily says: Zuzanna said, "I'm
inviting everyone except Emily
because she's a total pain."
So I just hid till they went.

 Bella says: But no one would
call you a pain, Emily. The
only girl who's a pain is Amy-
Lee.

Emily says; But she didn't
invite Amy-Lee, did she?

And then, at last, the little bit of puzzle clicks
into place in my head:

 Emily says: OMG. What if
she said Amy-Lee not Emi-
ly?!!!!!!!!!!!!!!!!!!!!

I cannot think straight. I was in the cubicle
and it was a bit difficult to hear and someone was
washing their hands and making a noise. Could she
have said Amy-Lee?

Oh, yes, she definitely could.

 Bella says: I keep telling you
to talk to her about it.

After I finish talking to Bella I have a good think. I don't know where the invitation has been but it doesn't matter any more. I should have just asked Zuzanna why she didn't invite me in the first place, then we could have sorted it out ages ago. It has been very hard work having a sworn enemy and it was all a waste of time anyway. Tomorrow I will totally have to explain it all to her.

I go into the kitchen. Mum is there, staring at the cooker like it is *her* sworn enemy.

"Having to make a different dinner every night is such a chore," she sighs. And I think she has only made one actual dinner in the last couple of weeks so she's getting off quite lightly really.

"How's Bella?" Mum says.

"Fine," I say. And then I think I don't actually know how Bella is because I didn't ask her. I just went on and on about me. I didn't even ask if Clover was better! I am beginning to think I am completely hopeless at being a friend.

Then I have one of my total flashes of creativityness. I will make Clover a card and I will write on it "Goat Well Soon". That will make Bella laugh.

I get my pens out on the kitchen table and fold a piece of card in half.

Mum says, "Who's the card for?"

"Clover."

"Clover?"

"Yes, she's not well. Bella's looking after her."

"That's nice," Mum says in the way that means she's already thinking of something else. Then she puts a load of knives and forks down right in the middle of my creative area.

CHAPTER TWENTY-SEVEN

Lots of Interesting People

Thursday

It is very fortunate that today Mum has got a cold – probably from walking to school in the rain – so Dad has to take me to school.

I still can't quite believe Chloe is not going to be there. It would be just like her to walk in and say, "You'll never believe it – it was all a dream!" or something. However I do not care about Chloe any more – I am excited to see Zuzanna. I know it sounds strange but I really am.

I will have to apologise for not inviting her to my party of course and explain, but I hope she won't mind. After all, she is very nice really, in fact I think we are quite similar, like Chloe said. I thought about making her a "Can We Be Friends?" card, but then I realised that was totally cringy, so I'll just have to be brave. I am so busy thinking that I am not really listening to Dad but as I get out of the van I hear him say, "... two weeks old today."

"Bye," I say, shutting the door, then I realise what he has just said. *Two weeks old!* The baby is two weeks old!

"You have to give her a name!" I call after the van as he drives off. "Anything! OR YOU'LL GO TO PRISON!"

I suddenly notice that everyone walking into school is looking at me.

"Don't worry," says a voice behind me. "If they behave they get out early. My dad was out in six months." Amy-Lee gives me what I think is meant to be a sympathetic smile as she walks off. I think I prefer her as a bully.

I look around frantically in case Zuzanna has heard but luckily she is not here yet. Thank goodness Gran is picking me up this afternoon (and I have never said that before) – at least she will know what to do about the baby name. Perhaps me and Gran can name the baby ourselves. "Agatha Hermione" might just have to do. Why is it that I never get to finish worrying about one thing before another thing comes along?

When I get into class everyone is talking about yesterday.

"Where's Zuzanna?" I say. But no one seems to know.

I go to my table. I have an empty chair next to me again. Chloe has not woken up to find it was a dream after all. I put Wavey Cat back in his place and push his paw so he starts waving. "Look, Wavey Cat," I say, "so far you haven't really done much of a job of this good luck stuff. Perhaps you are just new to it but if you would like to try with a little bit of luck today, I would be grateful."

Mrs Lovetofts comes in, all smiley of course. "Good morning, class. Well I'm sure you'll agree that was a lively day yesterday. Plenty of 'living history'. And some interesting archery displays." She gives me a little twinkly smile.

Mrs Lovetofts begins to call the register. When she gets to Zuzanna's name no one answers.

"Zuzanna?" she says again. "Oh no. Of course not." She goes back to calling names. What does she mean by "of course not"? Where is Zuzanna? She never has time off.

Mrs Lovetofts continues to call the register and everything seems like normal except . . . I am starting to worry. What if Zuzanna is not coming back? What if her mum is so cross about the Tudor trip that she moves her to another school? What if she got talking to Chloe's mum about Mag Hall and thought it sounded really good? I will have lost my third friend in four weeks. That is probably some kind of world record. My life is turning into a total friendship fiasco!

"Emily? Emily Sparkes?"

"Yes, Miss," I say.

All morning I am worrying and all morning there is no sign of Zuzanna. Although I'm not really sure what sort of sign there could be – most people are either in or not, they don't really bother with signs.

I try to ask Mrs Lovetofts why Zuzanna's not here but she just says, "Oh. It's just one of those things."

One of what things? There are *millions* of things! Has she been eaten by a rhinoceros? Moved to Jamaica? Maybe it's just something sensible like head lice. At lunchtime everyone wants to talk to me – about Chloe. I explain all about the wedding and Mag Hall.

"You could tell she wasn't going to stay here," Babette says.

"Yes, she was too interesting for this school," Nicole agrees (which is rather a surprise).

"We're all a bit ordinary, aren't we?" Gracie says. "We just don't do things like meet Jamie Oliver and have new swimming pools."

Joshua Radcliffe doesn't say much at all, he just looks a bit fed up and goes out to play football.

I take my lunch out to the ENDSHIP SEA. I need to have a think. Fortunately Mum has not put in any carrot sticks as it is impossible to think when you are eating carrot sticks, they make too much noise.

Zuzanna has still not turned up. I pull out the invitation. I just don't understand how it got into my bag without me noticing.

Then a very strange thing happens, *again*. A person comes to sit next to me and that person is – Amy-Lee.

"Found it then?" she says.

I quickly close the lid of my lunch box in case she tries to steal my Penguin.

"Found what?"

"The invitation. I put it in your bag."

"*You* put it in my bag?"

"Yeah. I put it in yesterday, when we got back from that Tudor place."

I don't say anything but I just give her a look that

says, "What were you doing with my invitation and why did you put it in my bag?" It is a very hard sort of look to describe.

"I didn't want to be the only one," she mutters.

"The only one *what*?"

"The only one who wasn't invited to the party. So I took your invitation."

"You took it?!"

"Yeah. Out of your tray. So you wouldn't get invited either. But then yesterday I was sort of thinking that you were OK really – you know, not telling Meakin about the Gary Barlow biscuits – so I gave it back."

"Right. Err . . . thanks," I say.

"Yeah," she says, looking at her feet. She doesn't say sorry because it's not the sort of word she's used to but I think maybe she means it a bit. She gets up to go and as she stands up I notice that the hem is coming down on her school skirt and that she is still wearing her sandals from the summer and I think maybe it is not that easy to be kind and friendly if your dad has been in prison and hasn't got a job.

"Hang on, Amy-Lee," I say. "If you want to go to parties, maybe you should start being nicer to people. You know, then you would get more people being nice back."

"Nice?"

I don't think that's a word she's very used to either.

"Yes. Like not snapping people's dolphin rubbers in half."

"Oh, yeah. That," she says and shrugs her shoulders and walks off.

Funny girl.

I have another go at thinking. I start thinking about friends and how they can be very confusing. Some people try to be popular by making loads of stuff up and some people want to get invited to parties and snap your rubber in half, but the people who are just nice and ordinary are really the best ones.

I go back into class and Nicole and Babette are there and I say, "It is not true that Chloe was more interesting than us. You are twins who speak French. You are very interesting."

And I say to Joshua Radcliffe, "You live in a yurt. You are very interesting."

And I say to Gracie McKenzie, "You have lots of brothers and sisters. You are very interesting."

And I say to Daniel Waller, "You are really sensitive. One day you might be a great artist. You are very interesting," and guess what, he doesn't cry, he smiles.

And then I realise that now Gross-Out and Alfie are looking at me and I think I might have started something I wish I hadn't. "And you two have . . . an unusual sense of humour," I say but I don't add the bit about them being very interesting because there have been quite enough lies lately.

I am doing well I think until I realise that Amy-Lee is waiting for me to talk about her.

"And you are very interesting because … because …"

"Because what?" Amy-Lee says.

"Because you don't let problems at home stop you getting what you want," I say. Which is one way of looking at it.

"Yeah," Yeah-Yeah Yasmin says.

I quickly go to sit down because there is *nothing* interesting I can think of to say about Yeah-Yeah Yasmin.

Then the bell goes and it is time for everyone to have another exciting afternoon of school. Mrs Lovetofts is just calling the register again, to make sure no one has got lost in the playground, when the door opens and in comes – Zuzanna!

I am so pleased to see her I say, "Hi, Zuzanna," really lots more loudly than is normal in class and everyone laughs. Zuzanna gives me a bit of a smile and goes to sit down. It seems like ages till afternoon break but as soon as the bell rings I go to find her.

"I thought you'd moved schools," I say.

"Moved schools? No, I went to the dentist."

"Your orange face is fading," I say.

"Oh, yes. I washed it loads."

There is a bit of a pause, and she starts to walk away.

"I found my invitation to Rollerworld!" I splutter.

"What?" Zuzanna turns back.

"The invitation to your party. I found it yesterday. Well, Amy-Lee sort of found it. I didn't get it, you see. I . . . I thought you hadn't invited me."

"Oh. I thought you didn't want to come." Zuzanna looks surprised.

"I wish I had come . . . and I'm really sorry I didn't invite you to my party."

"That's OK," Zuzanna says. "To be honest, after Mina left I didn't feel much like going to parties anyway," and for the first time it occurs to me how much Zuzanna must be missing her best friend too.

"Friends?" I say.

"Friends," she smiles. And I get a nice warm feeling inside.

After break Mrs Lovetofts comes to talk to us. "I just wondered," she says, "if you two girls would like to sit next to each other. After all, you do seem to be getting on well. Perhaps Zuzanna should come to sit in Bella's old chair."

Zuzanna looks at me and I look at Bella's place. Wavey Cat is grinning at me and waving his paw. I wonder how that happened.

"OK," I say, smiling. "If you want." And I feel Bella would smile too.

And she says, "*Totally*," and then we laugh. We go to get her stuff to move over to my table. Zuzanna picks up her bag and I get her pencil case off the table but then I see, right

in the middle of Zuzanna's table, an Ickwell Hall souvenir rubber.

"I thought you didn't get one of those," I say.

"I didn't," Zuzanna says.

"Well, it looks like you've got one now."

Zuzanna picks the rubber up and looks very pleased. I look around and notice Amy-Lee grinning across at us. Then she looks away quickly and flicks an elastic band at Joshua's head.

CHAPTER TWENTY-EIGHT

House Arrest!

Back home

Believe it or not, with everything that's been going on I had forgotten about my parents going to prison. It all comes rushing back though when I get out of school and see Gran's car parked outside. She has a grim look on her face.

"Have they been arrested yet, Gran?" I say as I get into the car.

"Not as far as I know. But we need to get this sorted out, Emily. That baby needs a name!" She grinds the car into gear and wheel-spins off down the road.

Even by Gran's standards the drive home is terrifying. I put my head down and try to remember some prayers but it is very difficult to concentrate with Gran swearing and yelling, "Get out of the way, you doddery old fool," to perfectly normal people trying to cross the road.

We pull up outside the house and I get out feeling very shaky. But we are only just in time as a police car pulls up behind us! I can't believe they got here so soon. They must have a nameless-baby detector car or something.

"Oh my Lord! They're here already," Gran says. "Leg it, Emily!" Gran pulls me up the path, shoves me through the front door and nearly falls in behind me.

"Mum!" I yell. "You're going to be arrested!"

"Arrested?" Mum says, coming out of the kitchen and wiping her hands on a tea towel. "Whatever for?"

"Where's Yoda!" I scream.

"Who?"

"The baby. They'll take her into care!"

"Over my dead body!" Gran says, slamming the front door and leaning against it.

"Will you all please be quiet," Mum says. "You'll wake the baby. She's having a nap. I've been having a bit of a tidy up. I *was* feeling much better."

Before I have a chance to say any more there is a ring on the front door bell.

"Don't answer it!" Gran says. "We'll say you're out. You can hide in the attic."

"Move out of the way, Mother," Mum says to Gran, and pushes past her to open the front door.

"Good afternoon, Madam," says a stern-looking policeman on the doorstep.

"It's all a bit of a mix-up, Officer," Gran says over

Mum's shoulder. "But we've sorted it out now. She's called Brenda Hermione."

"Is that your car outside, Madam?" says the policeman.

"Oh no," says Mum. "I have a Baby Eco-Jogger Deluxe."

"It's mine actually," Gran says.

The policeman frowns at Gran. "Well, perhaps you would be so good as to answer a few questions about why you were driving so erratically just now. You haven't been drinking, have you, Madam?"

"Drinking!" Gran says. "Don't be ridiculous. It's not Christmas."

"Ninety-one days," I add, but no one seems interested.

The policeman takes Gran outside for a bit of a telling-off and Mum says, "What on earth is going on, Emily?" Like it's got something to do with me.

I explain about the baby name and being arrested and going to prison and I say, "I have been trying to tell you about it but nobody around here listens to me any more!"

Mum sighs and puts her arms around me. "But you don't go to prison for not naming babies, Emily."

"But what about the two weeks?" I say.

"I don't know where you got that idea. You get at least six weeks, and even then you don't get arrested. Anyway you don't need to worry any more. We're going to call her—"

Before she can say anything else there is a squawk from upstairs and Mum goes up to get the baby. I go to put the kettle on. I know Mum doesn't like me doing it but I think it is time she realised I am growing up. I cannot believe how clean and tidy the kitchen is – come to think of it, the living room is quite tidy too. I think I might ask Zuzanna round for tea. I take the tea into the living room and Mum comes downstairs with the baby just as Gran comes back in too.

"He let me off," Gran says. "I explained there was a family crisis. And how is my little Brenda Hermione?" she says, tickling the baby under the chin.

"That is not her name," Mum snaps. "Look, if it makes you feel any better, we *have* decided on a name for the baby. Your dad and I had a little chat about it yesterday, Emily. We were going to tell you tonight."

"And about time too," Gran mumbles.

"It is a name that I have heard Emily mention a lot recently, and I thought it was very pretty. We thought we would call her Clo—"

"Nooooooo!" I interrupt. "Not Chloe! Please! I have heard that name quite enough. Perhaps we should go with Brenda – it's not too bad."

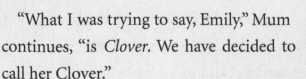

"What I was trying to say, Emily," Mum continues, "is *Clover*. We have decided to call her Clover."

"Clover!" Gran says, spluttering her tea. "Oh my stars! Whatever next?"

Mum ignores her. "You know, Emily? Like Bella's friend."

"Bella's *friend*?"

"Yes. The one you said was poorly and you made a get well card for the other night. It's a very pretty name. Don't you think?"

"Well," I say, "at least it's interesting."

And I'm sure Clover Sparkes smiles.

ACKNOWLEDGEMENTS

When you write a book only one person's name goes on the cover, but really a book is made by lots of people. I couldn't have written this book without the following people:

My very talented group of women writer friends whose support I draw on almost daily. If there's a writing problem that needs fixing, they won't rest till it's sorted (think Charlie's Angels, but with pens).

My three children for putting up with a thousand late dinners and missed school assemblies and for patiently accepting that Emily gets all the attention.

My lovely friend Amanda, for excellent coffee and for allowing me to harp on for hours about books and plots and contracts, never once letting on she has better things to do.

My amazing mum for unwavering support, countless babysitting and child collection duties and for always answering "Yes," when I say, "Can you help?"

The whole team at Little, Brown, especially my fantastic editor, Kate Agar, who has an instinctive understanding of books and stories but always manages to make me feel like I'm the clever one.

My super Special-Agent Gemma, who has more positive energy than a Duracell factory and is responsible for saying my favourite sentence ever, "So, tell me about this book you're writing . . ."

And finally my partner, Mick, for endless tea relays and for always believing in my dreams, even when I don't.

ABOUT THE AUTHOR

Ruth Fitzgerald was born in Bridgend, South Wales. She grew up in a happy, big, noisy family with far too many brothers.

When she was six years old she wrote her first story, "Mitzi the Mole Gets Married", and *immediately* announced she wanted to be a writer. Her teacher *immediately* advised her that writing was a hobby and she needed to get a proper job. Since then she has tried twenty-three proper jobs but really the only thing she likes doing is writing.

Ruth lives in Suffolk with her family, one very small dog and five chickens. They are all very supportive of her writing, although the chickens don't say a lot.

Think again . . .